A Wylder Homecoming

by

Evelyn Timidaiski

Wylder West Series

A Wylder Homecoming

Cover Art by *Kim Mendoza*

The Wild Rose Press, Inc.
PO Box 708
Adams Basin, NY 14410-0708
Visit us at www.thewildrosepress.com

Publishing History
First Edition, 2023
Trade Paperback ISBN 978-1-5092-4836-0
Digital ISBN 978-1-5092-4837-7

Wylder West Series
Published in the United States of America

She leaned in and touched her lips to his.

His pulse jerked and he hardened. Damn. How was he going to turn her down without hurting her more? When her fingers began an exploration of his chest, he grabbed her arm and held it with his.

"Ginny." His voice deepened to a growl. "You've got to listen, honey. You're not thinking straight. If you were yourself, you'd have already had my head for coming in here."

Her body jerked away. "Don't tell me what I'm thinking or not thinking. You're the boss but you don't get that power. Kiss me." She waited a heartbeat and said, "please?"

He knew it was wrong, but he couldn't refuse. Something in her face made him understand how tightly she was wound. He leaned in and pressed his lips against hers. Instantly, his control slipped a notch. When her tongue probed tentatively, he nearly lost it. He opened for her and let her explore. Fireworks exploded in his mind as she continued her search. Dear God, she was sweet.

She pulled back and looked at him in the faint light.

He placed his hand against her cheek, caressing, comforting.

She moved her mouth to kiss his palm. Once more she stared into his eyes. "I need you, Hayden."

Praise for Evelyn Timidaiski

A Soldier's Honor captured second place, Single Title category, 2012 Golden Gateway Contest, Unpublished Division:

"…If you're looking for an action military romance with emotional depth, pick up *A Soldier's Honor* today."

~ 5 stars, N. N. Light Reviews

~*~

Tiponi:
". . . a beautiful fantasy adventure, unlike anything I've read before. . . I found myself spellbound by the intricate mythology of the tribe the more I read. . ."

~ 5+ stars, N. N. Light Reviews

~*~

A Wylder Homecoming:
"…Timidaiski seamlessly marries the old west with modern technology . . . un-put-downable, especially for horse lovers and fans of the Wylder West series."

~Renee Canter Johnson

Dedication

To Jamesy with love

Acknowledgments

Authors may write a book, but they get help from so many people. I'd like to thank my family for their support and encouragement.
I'd like to thank my editor, Kaycee John, for her tireless help and endless patience with my errors.
I'd like to thank my cover artist, Kim Mendoza, for her beautiful work.

Prologue

Wylder, Wyoming Territory, 1870

Dirk Callahan pulled the collar of his Shearling jacket higher on his neck as he pushed the brim of his hat down on his face. The sheep skin lining helped against the cold but now, heavy wet flakes were beginning to fall. They would probably get a foot of snow by tonight. Pushing the thought aside, he tightened his grip on the reins. He thought longingly of the warm fire at home where his ma and pa would be sitting around the dinner table, eating a fine hearty stew and biscuits. He shuddered. That was all gone now.

This would be his last winter in Wyoming Territory. Pa had made it clear that he wanted a different kind of son—one who 'yes-sirred' and got up before dawn and went to bed as soon as he could drag himself there after a fifteen-hour day. Hell, with that. There were easier ways to get money. A half hour from now and he'd be rich. He wouldn't have a boss then—and no worries.

"Damn it's cold," Sam cursed."

Dirk gave the man a scowl. Sam was supposed to be quiet. He tried to think of the man's last name and couldn't. They'd met at a saloon in Cheyenne. Playing cards—and losing—wasn't the best way to find an accomplice to rob a stage but the man was older. At seventeen anyone older than yourself meant experience.

Dirk was ready and willing, but sadly lacking experience.

"Shut up!" he snapped. "They could be here at any minute."

"You said that thirty-damn-minutes ago. They're supposed to be here by now."

"Well, maybe they stopped for a shit for all we know."

Dirk wiped his forehead with the back of his gloved hand. There was no sweat—just nerves. He couldn't believe he was going to rob the stage from Cheyenne. He'd watched the coach pass the ranch as a kid and dreamed of going places. Warm places with no snow— exciting places like San Francisco or back East where he could wear fancy suits and smell something besides horse shit.

"What you gonna do first with your share?" Sam continued without taking a breath. "Me—I'm going to get me a real fine whore and the biggest steak dinner in the biggest hotel in Laredo."

"I told you to shut your trap. How do you expect to hear the stage with all that blabbering?"

"Just saying—hey, you ever had a whore, boy?"

"Does it matter? We're fixin' to rob a stage and all you can do is brag." Dirk cocked his head in the wind. "That's them." He pulled up his mask covering his face, gave a last thought to the warmth of home and pulled his Winchester from the scabbard. With the creak of leather and a shuffle in the saddle he readied himself.

"Remember, I do all the talking." Sam said before raising his own mask.

Within minutes the sound of the wheels from the stage could be heard, coming fast in their direction.

Dirk's gut tightened and his breath jerked through his lungs.

Sam said, "Wait until I shoot the guard before—"

"You never said nothin' about shootin' no guard."

"Dammit boy, don't be a fool. Do you expect them to just give us the money?"

Sweat beaded on Dirk's brow for real this time. He tried to swallow but couldn't. A whip cracked and the sound of the running horses raced toward them. This was one of the few spots rocky enough for them to hide. The coach had to be aware of this and sped up for safety. Just as they came even with the horsemen, Sam shot at the guard and missed.

If possible, the stage moved faster. Dirk and Sam took chase, firing as they rode. Sam's second shot took down the guard. As they sped up, Dirk fired at the driver and missed, but their point was made. The driver pulled back hard on the reins and brought the coach to a standstill.

Heart pounding, Dirk pointed his gun shakily at the driver. A hand reached out the window of the coach, a colt aimed at him. He shot and the hand dropped the gun. Not before sending a slug into his shoulder. It hurt like hell, but the arm was usable.

"Get down and unhitch the team," Sam growled and waited while the driver did as he was told. After the pin was released, Sam reached over and slapped the closest horse on the rump, sending the team on a flight of fear.

"Now, get up there and hand me the money." Sam moved his horse closer to the coach and peeked in. A female screech and a 'now hear there,' from a male occupant could be heard.

Dirk was nervous. Sam was paying too much

attention to the people in the coach. The guard was bad enough, but he couldn't stand by while his partner molested a lady. He edged his mount forward, but Sam moved between him and the money satchel. The leather bag made a thwack against Sam's chest as a bullet hit him in the back. He fell forward on his horse's back, managing to keep the bag safe and spur his horse onward.

Dirk's gaze flew to the guard who lay on the ground, rifle in hand. He didn't think but aimed and fired. The guard shot again and fell flat as Dirk's return bullet caught the man in the chest. Dirk now felt the burning coldness of a leg wound. Without blinking he took off after Sam.

****

Hours later, Sam fell from his horse, still clutching the money satchel. Dirk dismounted, canteen in hand. He helped Sam to take a sip of water, then watched the light go out in his eyes. He'd never seen anyone die before. Strange—he felt nothing. He was now experienced at robbing and killing. He had two wounds and was fast feeling the frigid cold seep into his bones.

Shelter. He had to find shelter, tend his wounds and warm up. Miles later, he came upon a rise of rocks, his heart accelerating at the thought of a place to rest. Removing the satchel, he got down from his horse and climbed unsteadily into the rocks. Weakness overcame him several times and he stopped for a panting breath. A sip of water and he continued to climb. On his knees, now, he crawled upward until it leveled out. He dug his fingers into the soft soil and pulled himself forward.

The ground gave way and he fell downward. He coughed to clear his mouth and throat, then swiped a bloody hand across his face. Faintly lit from the hole above his surroundings, it looked like a natural cave. He reached around frantically until his hand touched the money satchel. Thankfully he hadn't lost it in the fall. Laying back, he took a couple of breaths before deciding what to do.

Fire, that was right. He needed to get warm. Weary, though determined, he tried to sit up. Excruciating pain shot through his leg. His vision darkened and he nearly lost consciousness. He had to see what was wrong. Using his elbow, he pushed up and looked down at his leg. It was bent out of shape with a bone protruding from the front. *Jesus.* Tendrils of remembered Sunday school lessons raced through his mind. He'd never listened much but had heard enough to know—he'd drawn his last card and it wasn't good. Rest was what he needed. The chilling call of a wolf rattled his nerves. He settled himself and closed his eyes—for the last time.

Chapter One

Wyoming, Present Day

Hayden Wilcoyt scraped a hand across his stubbly beard as he drove down the pitch-black road. In the last fifteen hours, he had crossed desert, evergreen forests and now he was climbing the rocky hills of Wyoming. He couldn't be that far from the town, and he didn't want to sleep in another motel tonight. On the SEAL teams he had slept, or not slept, in some of the harshest conditions. But that was over now and here he was with all his earthly possessions in his truck, moving to a new state.

The argument he'd had with his dad had left a bitter taste in his mouth. They had always fought but this one was the 'I won't forgive you this time,' kind of fight. His father was estranged from the rest of his family, which made the discovery of a newly deceased great-grandfather an even bigger shock. Even stranger, he'd left everything, including a four-thousand-acre ranch, to Hayden. Hence his journey.

He saw the lights of a gas station off to the right. He'd better stop. The interstate might be the only place he could find gas in the small-town area of Wylder. After the inky blackness he'd been traveling through, the station was lit up like a New York arena. He pulled his truck in next to the pump. He stuck the nozzle in and locked it, then used his one-touch card to pay. As he wandered inside, his stomach growled. Grabbing two honey buns, some jerky, and an energy drink, he went to the counter.

"Hey, that's a sweet ride."

Hayden glanced at the disheveled looking teen and nodded. "It pushes the right buttons for me. How far is Wylder from here?"

The boy laughed. "It's about twenty miles up the road, but there's a cut off right next to the station that goes there. Are you the great-grandson?"

"How would you know that?"

"We don't get many strangers, especially those heading to Wylder so I figure you must be Wilcoyt's great-grandson who he left the whole show to," the kid said as he rang up the items. "If you're going to the ranch, you bypass the town. Just follow the road until it dead ends and turn left. Five-fifty, please."

Hayden paid, grabbed the bag with his snacks and went out to finish filling the tank. Moments later he was on the rough road beside the station, dodging gravel patches and praying he hadn't made a huge mistake.

He came to the dead end and turned left like the kid said. He saw only trees. After driving another eight miles or so, his headlights caught the shiny metal of a sign hung between two poles. *Wilcoyt Ranch*. He paused and flicked on the high beams. The fencing wasn't new, but it was well kept. As he turned through the gate, he tried to see some of the land. He parked on the bare dirt in front of an old ranch house. Not a single light shone anywhere.

Tired beyond reason, he grabbed his leather duffel and moved to the front porch. He knocked at the door and received no answer. He was a day early, but you'd think they would at least leave a light on. He grabbed the knob and it turned. Pushing inward, he stepped into a dark room and instinct kicked in just as the room lit up with a flash and the sound of a shotgun. He crashed into the hardwood floor. Without a thought he moved upward in a single athletic move and tackled whoever just shot him. Grabbing the gun, he threw it across the room. "Dammit to hell, you shot me!"

The person beneath him squirmed and kicked. He grabbed both their arms and yanked them up between muscular shoulders.

"Ouch, stop that. You're hurting me."

The sound of a woman's voice caused him to slacken his hold. "I'm not the one shooting at innocent strangers."

"Who came through my front door? Besides, I was aiming at the door. I really hit you?"

"I've been shot fifteen times. I recognize the feeling. Could you turn on a light if I release you? I don't want to hurt you, but I will if you don't cooperate."

"Whatever happened to my house, my rules?" Her voice was a little shaky but held a note of bravado.

Hayden sat up, releasing the woman. "It is my house."

He heard the sudden gasp of breath. "You're not due until tomorrow." The woman moved and flipped a switch. An overhead light turned on, shedding dim light but illuminating the room.

It was his turn to suck in a breath. Tall and lithe, the woman before him was Native American and beautiful. Her straight black hair hung down her back in a thick braid. He'd never seen a woman in coveralls but appreciated what she did for them. "I'm Hayden Wilcoyt, the new owner."

Her shoulders sagged and her face became less animated. "What the hell do you mean coming in here unannounced? I could have killed you." She looked at his bloody shoulder. "Oh my, God. I did hit you." Anger quickly turned into concern. "Come sit at the table. Let me have a look."

He eyed her warily and moved to sit in the chair. The sting of buckshot burned his shoulder. "I knocked and you didn't answer. Why were you sitting in the dark with a shotgun pointed at the door? Did you plan on shooting me with no questions asked?"

She grabbed his shirt and ripped it open. "You took about six pellets. I'll take them out if you can sit still. Let me get the first aid kit."

She hurried from the room, leaving him alone. The brief respite was needed to cool the hot flash of desire he'd felt along with her curves. He studied his surroundings to further cool himself down. The room was clean and neat, but nothing would help the nineteen-seventies decor. The orange and rust curtains and the multi-colored couch in the living room were a major flash from the past. What he saw of the kitchen was about the same. There wasn't a dining room, just a table in the kitchen.

She returned with a large toolbox filled with everything needed to take care of emergencies. He imagined there were quite a few cuts and scrapes to care for in the daily workings of the ranch.

"This is going to hurt but it shouldn't take long."

Her fingers probed gently around several of the shot marks. The pleasure of her touch vanished at the sting the of the alcohol wipes. The smell evoked memories of the numerous times he'd been stitched up. "You never answered my question. Who were you expecting to come through the door?"

She began to dig into his skin. "One of the vultures."

He bit his lip at the sudden pain. "I'm assuming you don't mean that literally."

"Since Austin died, people keep coming out of the woodwork wanting one thing or another. The worst was at the setting-up. Jason Lancaster came up beside me, right there in front of the casket, and handed me a paper saying Austin owed him a hundred-thousand-dollars. He said the ranch was collateral."

"What did you tell him?" Hayden asked.

An odd sound came from the back of her throat. A half-snort, half-growl. "Austin would never jeopardize the ranch for a loan. I kicked him out faster than rat shit and told him I'd shoot him if he showed up again."

Another pellet hit the bowl she'd set on the table.

"But you shot me instead."

"Are you whining?" She dug deeper into his flesh. "That's the last one." She dabbed at his skin with more wipes and covered the holes with gauze pads and adhesive tape.

"Are you Austin's ward?"

"What an awful word," she said. "I'm—I was his friend, Ginny Hampton. I've lived here for the last eight years."

His stomach growled loudly, interrupting the conversation. "Any chance of getting something to eat? My honey buns ran out about five minutes ago."

Ginny picked up the bowl and tossed the contents beneath the sink. She washed her hands, pulled out a clean bowl and opened the fridge. She filled the bowl from a plastic container and popped it into the microwave. Soon, the smell of beef stew made his stomach growl again. She grabbed two slices of bread from a sack and set the meal before him.

She sat quietly at the table as he ate. Unusual for someone who must have hundreds of questions. He used the bread to swipe the last of the stew from the bowl.

"Did you get enough? There's plenty more."

"I'm fine. Did you cook it?"

"That's me. Cook, cleaner, horse trainer and accountant. I've done it all since Austin got sick."

"I'll make it a priority to get you some help."

She snorted. "Like we can afford it."

"As soon as everything settles down, I'll see to it. As for money, I intend to make something special out of this place. I'm investing my savings and retirement, along with that of a friend's, in the ranch. So we can afford some extra help."

"A partner? Isn't that risky?" Her voice pitched higher with anger or fear, he wasn't sure.

"This place meant the world to Austin; I'd hate to see it lost in a partnership gone bad."

She didn't have to say it meant the world to her, too. It was in every line of her body.

Hayden had no intention of talking about his partner or their dealings. As much as Austin must have trusted her, she had yet to earn that from him. He didn't trust easily but once given; his trust was a bond. He stifled a yawn.

"You must be tired. I've cleaned Austin's room but if it makes you uncomfortable, there is a day bed in the office just over there." She pointed to his left. "Austin took naps there when he was too tired to continue working."

Hayden stood "I'll take the office for tonight."

"The bathroom is in the hallway. I wake up at five-thirty. Do you want to shower before or afterward? Unless you plan to sleep in. The men arrive at seven."

"I'm used to early hours, so I'll take mine at five."

"The towels are on the bathroom shelves." Without another word she moved down the hall to a room on the right.

Hayden looked around the dimly lit rooms. Shadows in the corners hid any further decor and made him anxious about morning. Regardless how the place looked, he was in it for the long haul. He only knew a little about ranching, but with his enthusiasm and hard work, he planned to make this a show place.

****

The noise in his ear wouldn't stop. Hayden reached for the portable clock and hit the stop button. With aching limbs, he rose from bed and headed for the bathroom. He didn't own a robe so in deference to Ginny he carried his jeans into the bathroom. The water in the shower came out fast and hot. Not what he expected in an old house like this. As good as it felt, he was conscious of how much hot water he was using. He turned off the steaming jets of water. They had made his muscles feel a little better but hadn't taken away the painful tugging of his scar tissue. He hurried to the office and quickly changed into clean clothes. Excitement hurried his movements. Today, he'd see the horses.

He pulled on his boots and grabbed his Stetson. It still looked new. He'd bought it two summers ago when he'd gone to Montana to help his friend Monte on his dad's ranch. He'd learned everything he knew about horses while recovering from two bullets to the chest.

Monte took one in the back during the same fight. Together they forged a friendship that would last a lifetime. SEALs were tight—brothers in arms. That's how his dream idea of creating a new breed of horses had been born.

His first glance of the ranch through the living room window nearly stopped his heart. Lavender and pink competed for center stage in the perfectly framed sunrise. He hurried through the door and leaned against the corral railing. The air smelled of earth, grass, and manure. It wasn't an unpleasant smell but one that intrigued him. He had such plans.

Ginny's husky morning voice pulled him out of his daydream. "Austin used to have his coffee out here every morning. He said it rejuvenated him."

The smell of coffee and bacon wafted to his nose and his stomach growled. He grinned. "You're going to think all I like to do is eat."

"Well, it's yours. Austin had the boys add that little shelf to the fence for just this." She placed the mug of black coffee next to a small plate of bacon biscuits.

"Thanks. You've made my day." He took a large bite of a biscuit and washed it down with the strong coffee. The coffee, food and view made quite a heady first memory of the ranch. He enjoyed a few more minutes of heaven and then moved to the house. He wanted to be inside when the men arrived.

He poured himself a second cup just as the door opened and two men came in. He gave them each a penetrating look before pulling out a chair to sit.

Ginny spoke, breaking the intense staring contest. "Morning, guys. This is the new owner and boss, Hayden Wilcoyt. Come sit down, I'm sure he has lots to tell us while we eat." Ginny placed the plate of biscuits on the table where they all but disappeared. She placed a bowl of sliced fruit in the center of the table with little bowls beside it. "There's oatmeal on the stove. As usual help yourself. "Mr. Wilcoyt, these are two of your hands. Ryan Petrie who lives in town with his wife, and Jeffry McCallister who stays in the bunkhouse. Where's Rick? He's usually here by now."

Ryan and Jeffry looked at each other and then away.

Ginny flashed a glance toward the door and back to the two men. "Spit it out. What are you not telling me?"

Ryan spoke up. "He quit. He said he needed more money. I think he's working on one of the ranches south of town."

"Just like that? No phone call or nothing? I thought better of him."

Hayden took in what was said, but more importantly what he saw. Ryan was upfront and honest. He figured he could trust this man. Jeffrey, on the other hand, wouldn't meet his eyes. A man who did that needed watching. "Morning, Ryan, Jeffrey. You can call me Hayden or boss. No misters on this ranch." He took another bite of biscuit and chewed. "In about an hour I'm going to want a tour of everything to see how things work. I've had some ranch experience, but I'm counting on you three to set me straight if I take a wrong step."

Jeffrey laughed. "If you step wrong around here, you're in horse shit." He hooted with laughter, and everyone joined in.

The tension broke. Hayden was about to speak when the door opened, and a giant of a man came in. Two black braids shot through with gray, bronzed skin, and high cheek bones denoted the man as Native American.

14

Hayden sat up straighter, his attention caught by the man.

The big man pulled out a chair across from Ryan and sat. "Morning. Sorry, I'm late."

Ginny spoke up. "This is Mustang Joe. We just call him Mustang. He's sort of my uncle on my mother's side."

"Mustang." Hayden nodded at the man. "I was just about to tell everyone that I want to see each of you separately after work. You can stop work a half hour early."

Mustang went to the stove and filled a bowl with oatmeal. "I've seen signs of the mustangs out by the creek on the north side of the property," he said to no one in particular.

Hayden gave the man a keen glance, liking what he saw. "Keep tabs on them, Mustang. I need them for the second part of my breeding program."

"They'll be here a couple of weeks, then'll go back up into the hills when the ranchers put out cattle. You want to breed the mustangs?"

"Yes," Hayden said. "I want to create a new breed by crossing mustangs with Morgans. He turned to Ginny. "Where are the books and when and how do the men get paid?"

Ginny and everyone but Mustang Joe got up. The others left as Ginny went with him back to the office. She opened the closet and pulled a key from a peg on the door back. "I have this year's and last year's books in the desk. The rest are in the closet. Sorry you have so little room."

"I'm fine. I'll work out a better bedroom later."

She handed him the key. "I've got to go. One man down and horses to feed."

Hayden felt a twinge of guilt at her statement. He

had to look at the books and see how bad things were. "Wait. When is payday and are the men's wages written down somewhere?"

"You'll find it all in the current year's book. Look, I've got to go."

"Why the big hurry? The horses can wait five minutes."

Ginny stared back at him with reluctance. "I… Jeff doesn't work as well when I'm not around."

"Slackers shouldn't be coddled. He'll be told today to get his act together or he's gone."

"You don't understand. It's hard to get people from town. They usually go to the factories over in the next county. All the college age kids are happy to kick the dust of Wylder off their feet and you can't blame them. There's nothing to keep them here."

"We'll work on finding a solution. Don't say anything to Jeff. I'll take care of it."

After Ginny left, he pulled the ledger closer. His gaze fell on the old desk. What had his grandfather been like? All the old scratches had been made by a man who had created his father and thereby him. He must have spent hours each night working on paperwork. He opened the book and looked at the handwriting. It was spindly and awkward. Flipping the pages, he came to another precise neat print. Ginny.

Somehow it didn't fit. She gave the impression of a wild spirit trapped inside a hardworking strong woman. Reading the entries was easy but tedious. As he got to the debt's ledger, he was appalled. The ranch was being run on a shoestring. How had Ginny done it? The figures looked fine at first glance but there was something off. He'd have to look at it in depth later. He closed the book and grabbed his hat. The horses were far more intriguing than numbers.

****

Dust billowed up from the wheelbarrow of manure and hay as Ginny shoveled another pile onto the heap. Damn the man. How could he come waltzing in here and start making ultimatums and calling for private employee meetings? In her eight years living here, things were never run that way. And why did he have such nice shoulders anyway? She'd felt the strength beneath her fingers as she'd probed his flesh. At that thought, she paused and wiped the sleeve of her shirt across her brow.

Ryan dropped the horse's hoof back on the floor and wiped his file on his leather apron. "Ginny, you better slow down. You'll wear yourself out."

"We're one man down and don't have time for talk. Where's Jeffrey?"

"He took Brandy out for her exercise. What's up?"

"All I can say is show your best work." Ginny leaned her pitchfork on the fence and picked up the handles of the wheelbarrow. "Bring Rebecca to the ring. She's the best we have."

Ryan walked to the third stall down and opened the gate. The mare lazily chewed the last bits of her food. "Come on, girl. Let's show him what you've got."

The horse was beautiful. Austin had bought her two years ago and had given her to Ginny as a gift. It was the only gift she had ever received. But that wasn't the only reason Rebecca was special. She and the horse had bonded the first time they'd met.

Hayden walked in just as Ryan started putting the horse at ease. Ginny pushed the wheelbarrow off to the side and approached him. "This is the main barn where we house all our mares."

Hayden leaned against the rail as the lights came on and Ryan led a beautiful copper-colored horse into the ring. Ginny watched Ryan run his hands down Rebecca's neck and back, then moved to her belly and legs. He removed her lead and snagged a coiled rope from the fence.

Hayden's usually serious face lit up. "She's gorgeous."

"That she is. Her name is Rebecca. We've had her two years and she's pregnant with her first foal." Ginny signaled to Ryan, then opened the gate. She and the new boss moved to the mare.

Hayden touched Rebecca's nose, letting the horse sniff him and learn his scent. "How many horses do we have?"

"We have six breeding mares and five work horses. We house the work horses in barn two along with our extra hay." Ginny leaned against the fence, watching Ryan put the horse through her normal warm up. "We have her entered in the *Wylder County Horse Show*, two weeks from now."

"Sounds interesting," he said. "I'll have to go, maybe take in the sites of Wylder."

"Actually, it's more than a simple horse show. Like the Wylder Fire Department Spring Dance. It slows traffic and fills every restaurant in town."

OMG. Was that her gushing on like a teenager?

"What are her bloodlines?"

She enjoyed discussing her favorite horse. "Her sire is Helsbore out of Trenton Farms. Rebecca is too small for their standards but she's perfect for breeding the kind of horses we sell."

Hayden looked around the barn. "Is there a reason we have so few animals? How can the ranch survive on what we have?"

Ginny's mouth turned down. She didn't like talking about money or the condition of the ranch. She'd worked hard to maintain the ranch on the little Austin provided. But the man—the new owner—deserved a response. She took a deep breath and said, "I don't really have an answer to that. Austin always seemed to come up with a little money here and there. He said he had put some away, but he didn't tell me where."

Hayden turned to face her. "What's the schedule for the horses?"

Ginny moved to the large feed dispensers on the wall. "First we check out each horse to make sure they're okay. You just saw Ryan do that with Rebecca. Each horse has a chart for everything. How much food and what kind. We mix their food and let them eat, then make sure they have water. After that they are let out into the paddock to graze while each of us works with training and exercising the individual horses. There's also the never ending but important job of mucking out the stalls. Late evening, we reverse things, and they end up back in their stalls. I sometimes do a walk through before bedtime.

"That's quite a regime. Work me into the schedule so each of you can take time off without it being a burden to the others. I'm counting on you to teach me the basics. My friend Monte will teach me about the breeding and selling."

"So, you're serious about this breeding program? "Her heartbeat quickened. She was excited about the opportunity to turn the ranch around but worried they might lose it in the process. She couldn't let that happen.

"I am. What's next?

"Ryan's getting her ready for the show. He's very good."

Hayden gave her an assessing look. "But you're better."

Heat rose in Ginny's cheeks. "I have a certain affinity with horses. I listen to them, and they do their best for me."

"I'm not sure about horse whisperers, but you seem to know your stuff."

Hayden moved forward and rubbed Rebecca's belly. "Won't there be a problem with her being pregnant?"

"We won't be able to show her much longer. Once she really starts expanding, she doesn't fit the criteria for the perfect show horse."

Hayden absorbed her words and realized there was so much to learn. In between working and learning, he had to make plans and put them into action for his breeding program. "Since he lives off the ranch, I'll talk to Ryan first. Send him over about four-thirty. You can go last since yours will take longer. Before I go back to work, would you show me where Austin's buried? I'd like to pay my respects."

"Sure, he's buried beside his wife by the big oak tree. He once told me he planted the tree as soon as he moved here to have a shady place to lie in the hereafter."

Hayden looked around at the sparse landscape. "Smart man."

He walked toward the back of the house and stopped under the large oak tree. There in a small, fenced plot were two graves. He wished he'd had the opportunity to meet the man. He probably would have liked him. They both had struggled to stay alive in a dangerous world. Austin had worked to make a success of his ranch and Hayden had fought to make a difference. His father sure as hell didn't possess any of the same integrity and grit. He said a quick prayer and went back into the house.

Once more he opened the books and tried to make sense of what was there. The numbers added up, but the income just didn't seem right. He had only known Ginny a few hours, but he'd stake his life on her honesty. She dutifully logged each entry down to the last penny. So, why was the ranch barely staying afloat. He flipped the page and came to the payroll. His blood began to boil. Both Ryan and Jeff were paid just above minimum wage. With the amount of work required and the value of the horses, the guys needed more pay. He looked through the entire book. There wasn't an entry for Ginny anywhere. She was working for free. He didn't look forward to their conversation tonight.

He heard her come into the kitchen, probably to start lunch. He went in and poured another cup of coffee. "Everything okay in the barn?"

The words sounded stilted, and he gave himself a mental kick. He'd been around all kinds of women but this one was different. She made him feel tongue-tied and awkward.

She hauled a large sack of potatoes onto the counter. "Right as rain."

Hayden decided to get straight to the point before he got distracted by her curves. "Tomorrow after feeding we'll go into town and take care of the bank matters and the Will. Is there somewhere we can have lunch?"

Ginny paused in taking the potatoes from the bag. "Maggy's has the best lunch in town. Maybe we can do the lawyer first. He likes to go fishing in the afternoons."

"You know the lawyer?"

"I know everyone in town. Wylder is small and you bump into each other at all the shops."

Hayden grabbed a carrot from the bag she had on the counter, using the crunch to avoid having to speak. She had him in knots while doing a simple task. Lifting the bags showed how toned her muscles were and the chopping...well, certain parts of her body swayed gently. Who would have thought chopping vegetables could be sexy. Maybe it was the way her jeans clung to her hips and nipped in at her waist.

Ginny spoke, interrupting his fantasy "Would you like to take a ride this afternoon? Trigger hasn't been out in ages."

Hayden pulled his mind back to the present. "We have a horse named Trigger?"

"Austin had one. He was a big western fan, and he had this beautiful Palomino. What better way to merge the two?"

"I haven't been on a horse since last summer. How are his manners?"

"Trigger's a gentleman most of the time though he likes to show his stuff occasionally. He just needs a firm hand. He's also the biggest horse we have, and you are not petite."

Hayden cracked a grin at the last part of her statement. "We'll need to pick up a few larger sized horses. Monte will need something to ride after he arrives."

Her jaw tightened as her hands chopped the vegetables in a frenzy of knife-work. Gone was the affable Ginny. In her place stood her evil twin. Unsure what to say he picked up his coffee and returned to the office.

Chapter Two

After lunch Hayden stood in front of Trigger who did a little dance as he tried to saddle him.

Ryan came out into the corral and stood, watching Hayden. "Need some help?"

"I got it, thanks." He wasn't sure what the others thought about his horse skills, but it couldn't be good. Finally, the horse gave in to his patience and he had the saddle on just as Ginny exited the barn on one of the mares.

He mounted the horse and held on while the animal jerked and pranced. He tightened the reigns. "Whoa, boy. Take it easy." The horse settled and he rode him around the corral to get the feel of him.

"I see you two have made friends," Ginny said as she rode from the stable. "He'll be a little frisky today, but if you continue to ride him daily, he'll come around."

"I bet he misses Austin."

Ginny's face turned somber. "Not so much. Austin had stopped riding this last year and a half. I usually take him out a couple times a week. It'll be nice having help with him."

"Which way?" he asked.

"I'll take the lead since I know the trail. We'll just go to the lake today since you're talking to the men later."

Hayden and Trigger settled into a nice pace as he followed Ginny who was on Ginger. Occasionally she'd drop back and point out something interesting in the landscape. The view was one of sage brushes, wildflowers, grasses, and pockets of different species of pine. The trees and shrubs were small because of the lack of rainfall in the steppe community. The grass would also suffer. He would need to set up irrigation for the fields in summer.

Without warning, Trigger screamed, then reared. Hayden scrambled to stay on the bucking horse but failed. As he met the ground, pain flared in his chest and abdomen. Ginny's horse also reared but she kept her seat and quickly grabbed her rifle. A single shot sounded before he had time to recognize the danger.

Hayden grabbed his belly and crawled into the low growing weeds for cover. He was pretty sure the bullet in his chest was a through and through but the wound in his gut was serious. The voice of his team leader sounded in his ear. "Nighthawk, do you copy?"

A barrage of bullets lit the night sky. The volley let him know that he was nearly surrounded. "Copy, but down. Need assistance."

There was a pause before the voice spoke again. "Copy, Nighthawk. Be ready in five."

Hayden crawled deeper into the tall grass. A hand on his shoulder sent him into defense mode. Grabbing the hand, he twisted it behind the soldier's body and reached for his knife.

"What the hell are you doing? Let me go." Ginny's voice, sounding anxious and pissed all at the same time, called him back to the present.

It took a few seconds for him to grasp reality before he released her arm and let her go. Wiping his wrist across his forehead, he noticed the beheaded rattler a few feet from him. Trigger had nearly stepped on the snake.

Taking the canteen from her saddle, she handed it to him. "Are you alright?"

"Yeah," he said and lumbered to his feet.

She stood and brushed down her jeans giving him a wary glance as she did so. "Were you having a flashback?"

Hayden stood silently. What should he say? If he told her about his flashbacks, she might turn away from him. If he didn't tell her, he might accidentally hurt her if she came upon him at the wrong time.

He decided on a pared down version of the truth. "I suppose you could call it that. I get spooked sometimes and remember when I got shot. I took two bullets that ended my career that day." He stepped back from her, allowing them both some space. "Listen. If you find me like that again, don't touch me. If I'd been wearing my knife today, you'd be dead. I'm a trained killer and I don't want you to get hurt."

He waited for the fear to bloom in her eyes. When it didn't, he took a closer look at her face. Instead of fear, he saw curiosity and concern. Silently he stood still, allowing her to look at him and see the killer inside.

After Ginny mounted her horse, she turned and looked down at him. "I'm not afraid of you and if you're waiting for me to run, you'll have a long wait. Now, if you're okay, let's circle the lake and head home."

Hayden found his hat and looked around for Trigger. "My horse seems to have deserted me. Are we going to ride double?"

"I told you Trigger's a gentleman. He might disappear while looking for the right clump of grass, but he'll come when called." She put her fingers in her mouth and let loose an ear-piercing whistle. Before she finished, he heard hooves coming around the bend. Momentarily, Trigger appeared but stopped about fifteen feet away. "He's still a little spooked. You'll have to gentle him before you get on him.

Hayden approached the horse cautiously and began rubbing him. Then, reaching into his pocket, he pulled out a couple of sugar cubes. The horse became putty in his hands. He mounted the horse and they headed for the lake.

Chapter Three

Supper was late because one of the horses was acting colicky. Since the mare was pregnant, they called the vet. Edith Sanderson arrived quickly. Hayden met her at her truck. He stuck out a hand and the vet dropped her painted-nailed hand into his. "Hello, I'm Hayden Wilcoyt. The new owner."

"Edith Sanderson. Glad to meet you. It's good to know someone is taking over this old place. Austin did what he could until he couldn't."

Hayden led the way to the barn where Ryan and Jeff hovered around a stall. Inside the stall Ginny ran her hands down Rebecca's flanks, whispering gentle words.

Edith slipped the rope from the gate but didn't go in. "How's she doing?"

Ginny moved to Rebecca's head, holding the horse still. "She's uncomfortable. I thought I heard bowel sounds, but I'm not sure."

Removing a stethoscope from her bag, the vet auscultated the horse's belly and then took the horse's temperature. "I hear enough bowel sounds and her temperature is fine. Did you change her food?"

"No. She's on a strict diet except for the carrots we give as treats."

The vet went to the feed trough and ran her hands through the food left in the bottom. "Do you normally add BBs to the mixture?"

"What the hell?" Ginny gasped. "I fed her this morning, and the food was fine. She normally eats every bite."

The vet shrugged. "Somehow she ate the metal." I'll give her banamine for now, along with a laxative. That will make her comfortable enough to transport. I want to do an ultrasound and monitor her tonight. With the pregnancy there's a higher risk.

Anger roiled in Hayden's stomach. BBs in the food was no accident. Someone had deliberately tried to harm the horse. Hurting animals was unthinkable, but he knew there were maniacs out there who got pleasure from a lot of things. He'd met them, too. The ones who liked to hurt and kill people.

The vet left with the sick horse in tow as the subdued group went to the house. Hopefully, Rebecca would make a full recovery at the vet's place. No one spoke as they ate the dried-out chicken for supper. Nothing could help its condition. Ginny would never leave a horse that wasn't well, so she'd had no time to rescue the meal.

"This was deliberate." Hayden's words jerked everyone to attention. "I want every bag of food checked before tomorrow's feeding time. Keep your eyes open for anyone showing up unexpectedly."

"Boss, how could that be?" Jeff protested.

"It had to be on purpose," Ryan said. "BBs are not manufactured around horse feed or hay."

"You bought new hay and feed today. Did you use it to feed the horses tonight?"

"We used the last of the food we had already," Ginny said. "And the supplies are still in the truck."

Hayden pushed his plate away and looked at Ryan and Jeff. "Don't open the bags, lock them in the storeroom, bring me the key. Ryan you can go home. Jeff you've got guard duty tonight."

Ginny forced the last bite of the dried-out chicken down. "You guys finish up and get started."

Ryan and Jeff picked up their plates, took them to the sink and left. Silent moments passed after the men were gone. Hayden leaned forward and patted her knee. "You know you're not supposed to get attached to farm animals. They're bought and sold and die. Your heart can be broken if you don't protect it."

"Are we still talking about horses? Has your heart ever been broken?" Ginny gave him a quizzical look. When his steely eyes met hers, she quickly dropped her gaze.

"Not really. I thought I was close a couple of times, but it didn't gel. My work made it extremely difficult to keep a relationship going. I never knew when the call would come, nor could I talk about where I went. It made trust a tricky thing. I finally gave up dating and settled for quick hookups. That didn't work either. There's a whole group of women out there who get off by doing Navy SEALs. I found it less than appealing and decided to go solo for a while. Then I was wounded and had to go out on medical. I'm physically sound, just not enough for the SEALs." He paused and gave her a lazy look. "What about you? Anyone special?"

She looked up at him with a disbelieving look. "If you can find a time slot on my card that's not filled with work, I'll arrange something." Her cheeks flushed a warm tint and she looked away. "I've got to help the men." She took off without another word.

Hayden thought about that empty card of hers. He wouldn't mind filling a couple of those slots. He heaved a sigh and pulled out his cell. He checked the wall by the kitchen phone and found what he was looking for. "Yes, I'd like to speak to the sheriff please. Someone tried to kill one of my horses."

****

Sun glinted off the windshield of the official vehicle pulling into the yard. Hayden watched the tall man exit. Placing his hat on his head, the man walked toward him. He didn't exactly swagger but looked stiff-necked and arrogant. He'd seen this man's type before. Give him a badge, a gun, and the power went to his head.

"Good evening. I'm Deputy Sheriff Mack Benson. You must be the new owner."

Hayden took in the exploratory gaze the deputy sent around the yard. He looked over his shoulder and caught a glimpse of Ginny leaving the barn. The deputy's face took on a predatory look. Something inside him tightened and coiled. He looked back at Ginny. Her face was flushed, and she looked hesitant. There was history between these two.

He stored that little tidbit away and turned back to the deputy. "I'm Hayden Wilcoyt." He didn't offer his hand and neither Benson.

"What's this about someone trying to kill your horse?"

Hayden heard the disbelief in his voice. "Someone put BBs in the horse food. The vet took the horse to monitor her overnight."

Benson took a notebook from his front pocket and flipped through the pages to a clean sheet. "Did anyone see the person who allegedly put the metal in the feed? Could be kids playing around."

Hayden hid his irritation, barely. The nearest house

was at least five miles away. Kids would need an incredibly good reason to come this far. "No, the vet found them when she was checking the horse."

The deputy wrote a quick note. "Could the BBs have gotten into the feed accidentally?"

Ginny snorted. "Mack, think with your head. We don't exactly keep BBs lying around near the horse food."

He had the grace to flush. "I'm trying to look at things from all angles."

Hayden smiled. Whatever history they had wasn't current. "It wasn't an accident. The BBs were only in the one feed sack. It's not a coincidence that she's our best horse. There has to be something you can do."

The deputy closed the cover and returned the notebook to his pocket. "Without a witness and little evidence, there's not much we can do. We don't have the manpower to watch over a herd of horses, even a small one."

Hayden bit back the word 'jackass' before it left his lips. He was new to the area and did not want to start out by making an enemy of the law. "Those horses are my life. I can't have anything happen to them. I'll hire men to guard the horses."

"Don't go getting a bunch of vigilantes. We don't want anyone killed."

Hayden had enough. Politeness had gotten him nowhere. "I'll do whatever it takes to keep my horses safe." He deliberately encroached on the deputy's space "If you're not going to help, keep the hell out of my way." He turned and walked toward the barn.

He heard Ginny speak to Benson. Her voice didn't sound placating, and the word 'jackass' came across loud and clear. The shadows in the barn were a welcome relief from the blazing sun. He grabbed a wheelbarrow and pitchfork. Mucking the stalls would provide a physical release if not a mental one from his constant companions of frustration and worry.

Ginny entered the barn, cheeks flaming and spine stiff. There was his other source of frustration. He needed to talk with her about the pull between them. He might try to pass it off as just sex, but somehow that didn't feel right. She intrigued him more than any of the other women who'd passed through his life. They temporarily scratched his itch but didn't tug at his emotions. Hell—what did he know about emotions. He had been trained to control all emotion. Sometimes it was hard to transition from ops to civilian encounters.

Ginny leaned on the stall across from the one he was working on. "I'm sorry."

Hayden stopped shoveling and leaned on the pitchfork. "What the hell do you need to apologize for?"

"Well—I mean, uh—

"Spit it out, Ginny. You've got no need to be afraid to speak your mind."

She pushed off from the rail and turned to face him head on. "I'm sorry Mack was such an idiot. He's basically a good man but likes to make himself out to be more than he is."

Hayden leaned the pitchfork against the rail and reached for her. "You can't take responsibility for everyone. Mack was intimidated by me. His reaction was to puff up and fall back on the badge. Men do that. I'm okay that we aren't going to be BFF's. As long as he does his job. How long were the two of you involved?"

"What do you mean?"

"I saw the signs. The two of you were romantically involved."

"My private life is private." With that, she left the barn, slamming the door behind her.

Ryan looked up as she huffed her way to the house. When Hayden came out three steps behind her, he grinned. "What did you say wrong this time?"

"I think I'm supposed to guess.

Chapter Four

Hayden's mouth tightened as Jeff slammed the outer door and left. The man hadn't taken his words of advice too well. Instinct told him Jeff wasn't totally trustworthy. The shirking of jobs and multitude of excuses all but announced his fate. Eventually he might feel forced to fire him.

Right now, with all the work and so much happening, it was all hands-on deck. Ryan's meeting went well. He was happy to be here, and the pay raise was much appreciated. Ryan also liked the idea of cottages for married men. That would give them a big pay boost plus keep them near in case of problems that arose.

Hayden threw down his pencil and took a sniff of the air. As a connoisseur of all kinds of pies, his nose told him there was cobbler in the oven. Before he could get up, Ginny walked in.

"That went well." Sarcasm dripped from her lips. "Did you fire him? Or did he quit?"

"Neither. I gave him a pay raise and a lecture. He didn't like the lecture near as much as the raise."

She leaned her back against the wall. "Is that sound business practice?"

Hayden swiveled around in the desk chair, looking up at her. "It's the way I do business. I lay down the rules, and the employee gets to choose to cooperate or not. Have you had time to look into hiring someone to help out with the house and kitchen?"

She shifted her feet. "Not yet. I'm working on it."

"Good, I need to talk to you about the books."

Ginny straightened and went on the defensive. "I don't make errors. Every penny is accounted for." Her chest rose with the deep breaths she began to take.

He tried to calm her. "I didn't say there was an error. There's something we need to discuss."

"If you don't like my method, I only copied how Austin did it."

"There's nothing wrong with the method, but there's a discrepancy."

If it was possible, she stood straighter. Her mouth tightened and the skin on her cheekbones got redder.

"I don't understand."

"Ginny, where did *your* money come from?"

Her mouth worked but words didn't come out. Finally, she spoke. "I used to take a salary just like the men. When things got tight and Austin no longer kept the books, I stopped taking one. If I needed anything I just bought it with the supplies."

"And didn't you need some for meals or nights out? What about new clothes?" Anger rose in his belly, and he shouted. "Did you not even take out something for the church on Sundays? My God, how could you live like that? As of today, you're getting a salary and a raise. Your pay is higher since you work with the horses and do things in the house. You pull the most weight around here."

She let out a huff and leaned back once more. "We're barely keeping afloat and you're worried about pantyhose and Sunday spending? I don't think you have any idea how sad things are."

Hayden took a calming breath before he spoke. "Your books are accurate, and I know exactly the dollars and cents left in the account. What *you* don't understand is I'm the new owner and my assets are now a part of the books. I promise you I can afford to pay you and some extra help." He got up and pulled his wallet from his jeans. He opened it, pulled five one-hundred-dollar bills from it, and put them into her palm. "Consider this last week's pay. Do some shopping when we go to town."

Her face was full blown embarrassed. "Is that all?"

"Just one more thing. You don't have to worry. We're not going to lose the ranch."

"And is that all I get to know? I've worked fourteen hours a day for years keeping this place going. Now, all I know is you're the new owner and I'm a paid employee. Don't I have a say in things?"

She turned and left him standing in the office. He thought back over the conversation and remembered several things he forgot to mention. Like the excellent job she'd done taking care of the place. And thanking her for taking care of Austin.

****

The next morning, Hayden grabbed a couple of sausage biscuits off the counter and poured himself a cup of coffee. He made a beeline for the fence to watch the sunrise. Moments later, he felt her presence beside him. His senses homed in on her fresh soap smell as she leaned against the rail beside him. He took another sip of coffee before turning to look at her.

"Morning," she murmured.

He nearly strangled as he took in her appearance. Gone were the coveralls and tee-shirt. In its place she wore a chambray shirt and a long, pencil-thin denim skirt. Her feet were clad in strappy red sandals which matched her tiny painted toenails.

She swirled her head and slung her heavy braid to her back. "Will I do?"

Hayden eyed the silver and turquoise belt buckle and matching earrings. He cleared his throat before saying, "You look beautiful. You realize we're just doing business today?"

"Of course. I enjoy dressing up when I get a chance. Besides, first impressions are important."

"You forgot one thing, my truck. You'll never be able to climb into the beast in that skirt."

"Should I change? It'll only take a minute."

"You should enjoy your day out. I'll figure something out." Hayden had a perfect vision of her wrapped in his arms, clinging to his neck as he lifted her into the truck. Oh yes. He liked the image.

"I need to grab my purse and I'll be ready."

He placed his cup on the fence shelf. "I'm going to check the barn. Meet me at the truck. Oh, and bring the paper Lancaster gave you. I want to check it out with the lawyer."

Fifteen minutes later they were in his truck, driving toward Wylder. Over her yelps, Hayden had lifted her in one quick motion and set her on the seat. The truck's suspension took the ruts with ease, so nothing interrupted their conversation. "What's the name of the lawyer?"

Ginny ran her slim hands down the sides of her skirt. "Malcolm Branson. He takes care of most legal business in town. You have to go to one of the larger cities if you have something complicated."

He slowed going through the gate and turned left.

"That might be the case if we have trouble with this Lancaster guy over the lien paper."

"What will we do if he's right? A hundred K will put a huge hole in your breeding program."

"I have a feeling it won't come to that."

The town appeared out of nowhere. There was no urban sprawl, just emptiness and then the town. Hayden spotted two traffic lights, a few clusters of buildings, and Wylder Street. Like most small towns, the activity was centered on main street.

Ginny pointed to an empty parking spot in front of a small two-story building. "Over there on the right."

Hayden pulled into the parking spot and cut the engine. "Are you ready?" He took in her now somber face. She kept wiping her hands against the denim skirt. "Take your time. I'm sure he'll wait for us."

She hesitated only a moment. "Let's get this done. I have to move on."

Hayden rushed around to the passenger side and caught her as she slid from the seat. She continued to slide down his body until her feet touched the curb. Her eyes widened and she stiffened. Neither, said anything but awareness stirred between them. Before he did something stupid, he stepped back.

A curly haired blond with luscious lips and lethal nails looked up from her work as they entered the office. "May I help you?" Her eyes traveled the length of his body, pausing at the broad shoulders, then his narrow hips.

He'd been checked out before but never quite so thoroughly. The woman's satisfied smile made him want to squirm.

Ginny gave the woman a slight smile. "We're here

to see Mr. Branson."

"Certainly," she answered while keeping an eye on Hayden. She picked up the phone. "Ginny and Mr. Wilcoyt are here. Yes, sir." She put the phone back on the hook and pointed to the stairs. "He said come on up."

They skirted the chairs and end table and climbed the stairs. At the top, a smallish man met them, clean shaven and gray haired. Behind his glasses, he eyed them with intelligence and openness. Hayden decided he liked him as he squeezed Branson's hand.

"Welcome to Wylder, Mr. Wilcoyt. Good morning, Ginny." He ushered them into his office and into two expensive leather chairs. "I'm so sorry about Austin's death, Ginny, Mr. Wilcoyt. I'll get straight to business." Reaching inside a desk drawer he pulled out a manila folder stuffed with papers. "Austin was a meticulous man. He died with all his papers in order."

He pulled out Austin's Will, looked at Hayden, then Ginny. "He left an acre of land to you, Ginny. The parcel is yours to choose and you also have a home at the ranch all your life. He thought you might want to build a little cabin one day."

The lawyer then turned to Hayden. "The rest of the property and possessions go to you, Mr. Wilcoyt." From inside the folder, he pulled out a key and handed it to Hayden. "This is his safety deposit key. The box is in the bank down the street."

Hayden picked up the key, the metal cool on his skin. How many times had his great grandfather held this? What kinds of things would he deem worthy of the expense of the box? "Thank you, Mr. Branson. There's another matter we wish to ask you about.

Ginny pulled the lien letter out of her purse and

placed it on the desk. "Jason Lancaster handed this to me at the wake. He said if I didn't pay up, he'd foreclose on the property."

The lawyer took the paper and carefully examined it. "I'd have to see the original to be sure, but it looks legal. Austin never said anything about a loan. That's out of character for him. He liked to pay, and get paid, in cash. I'll look into this. If there's a problem, I can give you the name of a top-notch attorney in Cheyenne."

Hayden slipped the key into his pocket. "We appreciate your help."

"I almost forgot. Since your signature isn't on the safety deposit box, you'll need this letter to get access." Branson handed the envelope to Hayden. "Just a word of advice. Lancaster is a dangerous man. He's been buying up all the property he can. I have a hunch he has development in mind. Watch your step."

****

The bright sunlight was welcome after the dim interior of the building. Hayden placed a hand on Ginny's back as they moved down the sidewalk. "You're awfully quiet."

"What can I say? Everything was spelled out quite clearly."

Her voice rang with hurt. Hayden knew it wasn't the money. Ginny didn't care about money. She was hurt because Austin had barely acknowledged her. He decided to hold his counsel until they were eating lunch. Ginny stopped in front of Maggy's Diner. Its appearance made one aware of the limited choices for eating in a small town. He opened the door for her and stepped in behind her. The sound of dishes clanging together, twenty or more ongoing conversations and the smell of fried food greeted them.

Ginny moved quickly to the only vacant booth in the place. Cowboy attired patrons brushed shoulders with women in smart dresses and men in suits. Maggy's was definitely the hot spot in town. A young server stopped and filled their glasses with water. "Morning, Ginny." The girl of about seventeen flashed him a smile. "Who is the handsome stranger?"

"Hi, Rhonda. This is Hayden Wilcoyt, the new owner of Wilcoyt Ranch. How's school?"

Rhonda handed them menus. " Just two weeks until graduation and then I'll work here full time until I go to university in the fall. I can't wait to leave this place. Family is nice, but I want to see the world."

Ginny cast Hayden a 'see, what did I tell you' look. Their glances met and held. The look was a few seconds too long and Ginny blurted, "I know the menu by heart. Do you trust me to order for you? It will save lots of time if I give her the order now."

Hayden nodded and took a sip of water.

Ginny gave Rhonda the order and sat back and relaxed. "What do you think?"

"It smells wonderful, but I never judge a diner by smell alone. How do you feel about the Will?"

Her bright look faded along with her smile. "I knew Austin wouldn't leave the ranch to me. He was too old-fashioned and traditional. He would have thought that I couldn't handle it because I'm a woman. He also wouldn't leave it to someone who wasn't related. He was a firm believer in blood inheriting."

"That's strange because my family has been split apart for as long as I can remember. I didn't know my uncle much less ever hear of a great-grandfather."

Ginny grabbed a pack of crackers from the plastic bowl and began to nibble. "He knew about you. He mentioned you a time or two but never said much. I had no idea if you really existed or anything about you."

"Why didn't he contact me? I would have loved to have someone I could care about."

"Austin was stubborn. Whatever happened between your father and him would have been hard to mend."

He opened his napkin and unrolled his silverware. "I suppose I can relate. My father and I had a final row the day I left for Wyoming. I don't think I can forgive him."

"You're young. Maybe one day things will improve between the two of you."

Hayden frowned. "I doubt it. Coming from one of such tender years that sounds like an old soul. Do you have an old soul, Ginny?

She looked down at her hands where her fingers were crushing the paper wrapper. "I sometimes feel I was born old. Of course, running away from home at fourteen ages a person."

Hayden reached across the table and took the wrapper from her tightly clamped fingers. "Want to talk about it?"

Her response came out clipped and sharp. "It's a closed chapter in my life."

Rhonda returned with their food. "Bison burger for you, sir, and your usual salad, Ginny."

Hayden made a quick comparison of the burger and the salad. "Are you sure you don't want something more substantial?"

Ginny's laugh sounded so natural. He listened and grinned. "This is just what I want. I spend quite a lot of time trying to disguise vegetables so the men will eat them. Anytime I'm away for lunch, I indulge myself."

"You can plan as many vegetables as you want. The guys can eat it or not. You spoil them."

"I suppose I do. I know they don't make that much. The least I can do is feed them well."

Hayden filed that away for another conversation and took a nice juicy bite of his bison burger. Ginny dug into her salad, and they enjoyed a few restful moments as they ate. He set his burger down and dredged a fry in copious amounts of ketchup. He searched around for a topic that wouldn't cause her more distress. Austin's will had dealt her a blow whether she wanted to admit it or not. "What do you know about the banker?"

She put her fork down. "I just keep my money there. I haven't had any dealings with Mr. Gilbert, the owner or manager of the bank. You'll need to deal with him because of the letter."

"Hopefully, there will be no problem. What about Lancaster? You shared your experience, but what's his position in the community?"

"He's not well liked. He moved here about five years ago and has been buying up ranches right and left. Like the lawyer said, he's probably looking to develop."

He popped the drenched fry into his mouth. "I know one ranch he won't get his hands on."

"How can you be so sure? What if Austin did take out the loan?"

"I didn't know Austin, but I know his kind. If he had made a loan, he would have paid it off. The old breed didn't believe in owing anyone."

She took a bite, chewing silently. Her brow remained creased in a frown.

"Look, Ginny, I would take a hit if the loan *was*

legit. Between Monte and me, we've more than enough to cover the loan and continue building the breeding business. Austin isn't here to find little bits of money here and there to keep the ranch going like he did in the past. Have a little faith in me. I don't quit."

"Good. The horse business is not for the faint of heart."

Hayden caught the server's eye. "Check please."

Chapter Five

The bell on the door chimed behind them as they stepped back into the sunlight and silence. Though it was main street, there was little activity and no traffic. Hayden guided Ginny down the street to last building on the right. The sign read, Gilbert Bank. It looked as if it had served the town a few decades. They entered and encountered the typical bank setup. They went up to a window.

The perky teller gave them a welcoming smile. "How can I help you today?"

"I'd like to speak with Mr. Gilbert, please."

"What is your business, sir?"

"I'll speak to Mr. Gilbert about that. Tell him I'm the new owner of Wilcoyt Ranch."

The woman's smile brightened several watts. "I'll let him know. If you'll just have a seat, he'll be right with you."

Ginny sat on the edge of her chair as he crossed his foot over his knee. Two heartbeats later, a middle-aged man came from one of four offices. "Mr. Wilcoyt, I'm so pleased to meet you. Good afternoon, Ginny. Come this way and I'll personally take care of you."

They sat in the two chairs, facing the desk. "I have a letter from Austin's lawyer. I understand there is a safety deposit box. I'd like to retrieve his things. As you can see in the letter, I inherited everything."

Mr. Gilbert cast a quick look at Ginny, then looked down at the letter. "It seems to be in order. Do you have the key?"

Hayden removed the key from his pocket and set it on the desk. "I also need to start an account."

A smile spread across the banker's face. "I'd be happy to help. Come this way."

Hayden looked at Ginny. "This is going to take some time. Why don't you go take care of your shopping? I'll meet you back at the truck."

He watched her mouth tighten and her fingers pressed deeply into her purse. "Of course. I'll see how much damage I can do with my pay."

He smiled at her dig. She wasn't giving in easily to the matter of a paycheck.

Mr. Gilbert inserted both keys into the lock and opened the door. Pulling a large box from the slot, he placed it on the table. "There's a private, windowless room just to your left. Ring the bell if you need anything." He turned and left.

Alone, Hayden picked up the box and entered the claustrophobic room. He sat and stared at the box for several moments. It felt like a sacrilege to go through a dead man's possessions. He ran his fingers down the edges of the box before opening it. He got a whiff of good cigars and old paper, but it was the smell of gun powder that came as a surprise. As he riffled through the envelopes and photos, he uncovered an old Colt .45. His hands itched to touch it, but he opted to look through the rest of the box first.

There were two thick envelopes, one bearing his name, the other had Ginny's. Each had the flaps folded in but were not sealed. He wiped his damp hands on his jeans before opening the one bearing his name. It was filled with a thick stack of one-thousand-dollar bills. He quickly counted, whistling when the total came to two-hundred-fifty-thousand dollars.

This was where Austin hid his money? But why when the ranch was barely eking by, and all this money just sat in the box. He looked again and found a single folded slip of paper. Scrawled across the envelope in the same spidery handwriting he recognized from the books, he found his name. He traced the curled letter H. The hair stood up on the back of his neck. The note read:

Dear Hayden,

I regret we never got the chance to meet but some wounds can't be healed. I'm proud of the man you have become. You've done a job few can do and even fewer can do well. I've been saving for years to buy a prime stallion. I hope you'll buy one and maybe find your dream. Watch over Ginny for me.

Austin

Hayden blinked and quickly folded the sheet. Sliding it back in the envelope with the money, he picked up the next one with Ginny's name on it. Since it wasn't sealed, he opened it to find another folded note and fifty-thousand dollars. Between the two envelopes there was over a quarter-million dollars. He hadn't expected this. With this money and his seed money, he should have plenty to build the business. He fingered the note but slipped it back into the envelope unopened. He'd invaded Ginny's life enough. Austin's words to her could remain private. Pushing the envelopes to the side, he picked up the gun. Heavy and unwieldy, it intrigued him. He'd love to hear the story. The rest of the papers would need to be gone through but not now. He'd take it all home and go through it there. He rang the bell and asked for a bag to put the contents in. As he left the bank, he tried not to feel self-conscious knowing he carried a gun in the bag.

Ginny wasn't at the truck, so he locked the bag inside, deciding to look around. He passed the typical shops found in small towns and a few specialty shops that carried jewelry and local crafts. Passing those, an old newspaper clipping caught his eye in the window of a small museum. He paid the ridiculously small fee and added a twenty to the donation box. He passed displays of old six-guns and buckskin clothing.

Rounding the corner by the window he found the rest of the display. *Stagecoach Robbed!* The headline took up a goodly portion of the paper plastered across the window. An old stagecoach sat like a faded ghost in the shadows as the buckskin clad mannequins stared off into space. He dutifully read the newspaper and marveled that the robbers had never been caught.

"Pretty neat story," said the man from behind him. The name badge on his denim shirt proclaimed him the curator of the small museum.

Hayden walked over to look inside the coach. "I wonder if the money was lost or spent."

"According to legend, it's hidden around here somewhere. People have been looking for it for years. The Wilcoyt Ranch sits on the area the stagecoach was robbed. Some people think the money was hidden nearby. They found the body of one of the two robbers. The other was never caught."

Hayden took that bit of information and tucked it away. Treasure hunters might try to harm his animals. But what would they gain? He finished touring the rest of the museum and headed back to the truck.

Chapter Six

Ginny stepped from the door of the salon with a smile on her face. A facial and deep conditioning hair treatment went a long way to improving her mood. Her usual regime of moisturizers couldn't compete with the session she just had. The price tag had made her cringe until she remembered her argument with Hayden. Silly to complain about receiving a salary for something she'd done for years at no pay, but her frugality came from years of doing the best she could.

Hayden waited by the truck. As she approached, something changed in his eyes. They narrowed as they followed her path to the truck. As she got closer, she recognized the heat within them. He wanted her. The thought both excited her and freaked her out. Having a fling with the boss wasn't in the cards.

She tossed her bag into the truck and waited as Hayden lifted her into the seat. Why couldn't they have taken her car? It was ratty but at least she could get into her own seat. His arms were all corded muscle which made her heart miss a beat. Hopefully he'd think her hot cheeks were from the temperature in the truck.

"It's too far to walk in this heat. Take Old Cheyenne Road and turn left over the tracks. Lancaster's Land Company is behind the telegraph office. We really should have made an appointment."

"If we miss him, we'll come back tomorrow."

"Just like that. Small towns work on their own schedule and taking half days on Mondays or Wednesdays is common." She pushed an annoying strand of hair behind her ear.

He made the turn, drove over the tracks and pulled into an empty spot. "It's been my experience that money talks. If he thinks he has a chance of collecting on that paper, he'll make himself available."

Ginny clamped down on her comment. Hayden looked to be a gung-ho kind of guy. Hopefully, he was right.

The interior was bright and cool as they entered. She moved to the desk and gave the young blond-haired woman a smile. Her eyes hidden behind designer frames opened wider. *Damn,* Ginny thought. The woman wasn't even looking at her.

"You must be the great-grandson. Welcome to Wylder. How may I help you?"

Ginny felt Hayden's comforting form when he stepped up beside her. "We'd like to see Mr. Lancaster, please, "she said.

The woman looked over her glasses in contemplation of Ginny's interruption. "Do you have an appointment? Mr. Lancaster is a busy man."

Hayden leaned in, offering a dazzling smile. "I think he'll want to see us, Ms. Parks." He turned the nameplate to Ginny's view.

The woman responded either to her name or Hayden and rolled her chair back. "I'll see if Mr. Lancaster is in." She walked with sashaying hips toward a back office. Moments later she motioned from the hallway for them to follow her.

As the receptionist showed them into a well-appointed office, a male voice said, "Get some coffee started, Lisa. Bring me the Wilcoyt file. And step on it."

Inside the office, a man stood from behind a carved wood desk the size of an airplane carrier. "Jason Lancaster," he said and looked at them like they were best friends. "Won't you sit down, Hayden, Ginny." He indicated the two empty chairs in front of the carrier.

As they sat, Ms. Parks rushed in with a slim file folder.

"Hold my calls." Lancaster threw the comment at the woman's back as she rushed back out the office. "How can I help you today?" He didn't offer a hand; neither did Hayden.

Ginny swallowed hard to prevent the bile from coming up into her throat. The man was so ingratiating when she knew him for the snake he was. She cut her gaze sideways and couldn't read a thing on Hayden's face. He'd make a great poker player. He looked open and ready to do business.

He started off with, "I understand you approached my employee at the viewing of my great grandfather."

Ginny bit her tongue at the use of the word employee to describe her. Technically, it was correct, but it stung to be placed on a lower status. She'd always been the one who met the ogres and protected Austin from them. He had a new protector now and she had to live with it.

"I did indeed." Lancaster put a serious look on his face. "I'm so sorry for your loss."

"Thank you," Hayden said in a clipped, no-nonsense tone. "I want you to know I don't like it when people bypass the boss and go to someone else when it's my business. Don't go to Ginny ever again about the ranch.

She no longer has any reason to deal with the business end of things unless I say so."

Feeling the tire tracks running up her back, Ginny fumed. Hayden was coming on as a hard ass, but did he have to trash her in the process?

"Now just a minute," Lancaster blustered. "I had no idea you would inherit part of the ranch. I thought Ginny would get everything, so I approached her."

"At the viewing, when she was emotionally fragile?" Hayden asked. "That was unkind to say the least."

"Just where do you get off telling me this? I own a lien on Wilcoyt Ranch. I could call it in at any minute." Lancaster straightened in his chair and tried to stare Hayden down. He looked away first.

"For the record, Ginny inherits nothing. I get everything."

For one of the first times she could remember, Jason Lancaster looked uncomfortable. "Are you just going to kick her out?" he sputtered.

Hayden leaned forward a little. "I'd like to see the files you have on the alleged lien."

Lancaster slid the thin folder across the table. "Here."

Jason Lancaster was nothing if not cagey. Ginny pulled the lien paper out of her purse and handed it to Hayden. She wiped her hands on her skirt afterward. Just touching the paper gave her the willies. She wasn't sure what Hayden had planned for this turn of events. There in the folder lay the original copy of the paper she held.

Hayden took the sheet and compared it to the one he had. "Where's the rest of the paperwork?"

Lancaster's demeanor puffed up. "What do you

mean? That's all I need."

"I'd like to see the other paperwork with the terms of the loan and original paperwork."

Lancaster tried to stare Hayden down. Once more he lost. "Lisa, bring the other files," he bellowed. Before the words were completely out of his mouth, the woman entered and placed three thick folders on the desk. Briskly he handed Hayden the top folder.

Hayden flipped through the pages and ran his thumb across the signature at the bottom of the last page. "I see two things that bother me. One, this is a copy. Two, the loan is not with Lancaster Inc. It states that Austin took out a loan more than twenty years ago with the National Bank of Cheyenne."

"I bought the loan from the bank. It's legal and done all the time."

"Could I see the rest of the files?" Hayden's voice was calm, yet the request came over as a command.

"You'll need a court order to see the rest."

Hayden closed the file and placed it on the desk as he stood. "My lawyers will be in touch."

Ginny hastily stood and walked with Hayden toward the door.

"I can't wait," Lancaster thundered.

They passed Ms. Parks, who held a carafe and three cups on a tray. Ginny took a good whiff of the coffee and had the fleeting thought of drinking a cup. Another bellow came from the back office. Ginny turned away without a backward glance and exited the building. Once outside, she took a cleansing breath.

"I think we have him on the run," Hayden said as he helped her into the hot truck.

"I want off the track, please. You two play hardball.

I'll stick to horses." She buckled up. "What do you say we roll the windows down and let the wind blow the cobwebs out? I feel like I've been run over by a semi and then dragged around the track a time or two."

"I think that's a great idea. Dibs on the music." He grinned and cranked up the vintage rock and roll station.

****

Back at the ranch, while Ginny worked in the barn, Hayden sat in the office. He pulled out the sac containing his great-grandfather's belongings. After checking the handgun for safety, he returned it to the bag, then picked up a small leather pouch. Several rocks fell out onto the desk after he opened it. Curious, he studied each of them but couldn't understand why Austin would keep them in his safety deposit box. Just as he started to put them back, he noticed a crumpled piece of paper at the bottom of the pouch.

He saw a crude map. Of course, he recognized none of the places and landmarks. He'd have to wait for the right moment and ask Ginny. Checking the time, he put everything back in the desk and locked it. He'd have to get a safe for the house. A ranch always needed money on hand to pay for temporary help and other essentials. Looking around the crowded office, he felt frustrated. The office needed more space, and he needed a true bedroom.

Maybe he should check out the attic. He really didn't want to stay in Austin's room. He'd removed everything the old man had owned and taking over his grandfather's bedroom bothered him. Though he had never known the man, he didn't want to take something so personal. He'd bet his last dime, Austin wouldn't like it either. He needed to put some distance between himself and Ginny.

Slamming the door on that thought, he went in search of the egress into the attic.

He checked through the house and got nowhere. The only other place was Ginny's room. He hesitated for a second and visualized what Ginny might do if she knew he'd entered her private space. Hell, if he was careful, she'd never even know he'd been in there.

Slowly, he turned the knob and eased the door open. Her smell permeated the room. The light floral and spice scent entangled his normally clear-thinking mind. He flipped the light on and looked at the tidy room. Her personality was stamped all over it. From the paintings of wild Mustangs, Native American artifacts, and a Bible on the table, the room shouted Ginny.

"What are you doing in my room?" she gasped, horror in her voice. "Are you some kind of pervert?"

Hayden flinched inwardly. No one had ever called him that. "Now, just wait a minute. I have a perfectly good reason for being in here. I'm looking for the entrance to the attic."

"Couldn't you have waited for me to come in to fix lunch?" Her voice had come down an octave but still held some challenge.

He turned around in the small room, looking at the ceiling. His frustration doubled now that he was a little embarrassed. "Where the hell is the opening?"

"It's in the laundry room. The opening in the ceiling blends into the molding. Why do you need to get into the attic?"

Hayden edged toward the door, putting more space between them. She helped by moving to sit at the small desk. "Do you mind showing me? There could be papers stored up there and if it's large enough, I can put a bedroom upstairs." She started to say something, and he interjected. "I really wouldn't feel comfortable in Austin's room. The office needs to be larger and public. Privacy is an issue as far as bedrooms go."

"I don't remember him putting anything in the attic since I've been here. He usually just stuffed things in the desk or the filing cabinet. There is a window up there, so the ceilings could be high enough for adding a room. I'll show you the exact spot. There's a ladder in the storage closet."

Hayden got the ladder and followed her down the hall. He breathed a little easier now that he was out of the confines of her bedroom. Thoughts of doing more than talking in that room caused him to shift his jeans a little for comfort.

"It's in the center along the back wall." She pointed at the spot, her voice rang with disdain. "Do you need me to hold the ladder?"

"No thanks. I've got it."

"I've got more to do in the barn. I'll see you tonight."

He stopped her as she turned. "Do you have any leads on extra help?"

"Yes, I have two girls coming out tomorrow for interviews, unless you want to do that."

"No, you can do it. You'll know more of the details."

He watched her walk back down the hall, admiring the fit of her jeans. Dammit. Maybe he *was* turning into a pervert. He set up the ladder and pushed the cover up and into the attic. He found a string hanging from the ceiling; one tug turned on the light. No one had been up here for years. Layers of dust covered old furniture and stacks of boxes.

His attention zeroed in on the boxes. Hopefully,

some of these contained papers. Opening the first one, he was rewarded with stacks of files. When he checked out the other boxes he found more of the same. He wiped sweat from his eyes and took a good look around. The ceiling was high enough for him to have plenty of headroom. The window was small but looked out onto the front paddock. It would catch the morning sun. He wasn't an architect, but he thought with dormers, larger windows and air conditioning, it would make quite a nice master bedroom. He'd need to put on an addition for a bathroom. He took one last look around and headed back down.

Chapter Seven

After Ginny finished the last of the dinner dishes, she turned to go to her room. Hayden stood by the coffee pot directly in front of her. She nearly bumped into him. "Sorry, I wasn't paying attention."

Hayden poured the last dregs from the pot, then rinsed out the pot before he answered. "I'm sorry I invaded your privacy today. I didn't mean it as an intrusion."

She heard the sincerity in his voice and felt a measure of relief. "It's just that Austin was such a private person. I felt more comfortable in my room or the stables, the only two places that don't bear the stamp of his personality."

Hayden touched her arm, then pulled his hand back when she gave a slight jerk. "Did Austin make you feel uncomfortable?"

"He was at all times a gentleman. He never made advances and I wasn't his mistress. There's been plenty of gossip about us over the years. There was no truth in the stories."

"I didn't mean to imply—"

"I'm sure you wondered. A girl of twenty-two living with a ninety-six-year-old man. Everyone is bound to add two and two and get five."

Hayden took a gulp of coffee and Ginny watched the muscles in his throat as he swallowed. He looked at her and she knew the moment he became aware of her. Not as Ginny the ward of his great-grandfather, but as a woman. One that he was attracted to.

She broke the spell that had aroused both. She could feel the heat from his body, and it was driving her mad. "I should go."

"You're forgetting," he murmured in that sexy voice, another thing about him that made her skin itch. "We're supposed to talk tonight."

"Oh, what do you need to say to me?"

"You didn't see the contents of the safety deposit box. There's something in it for you."

"For me? I thought Austin left me an acre of land."

"He did, but there's more. Let's go into the office."

Hesitantly, she followed him. What did he have in mind? She took a breath and entered the room. They had their differences, but she knew she could trust him. She was more worried about trusting herself. She was attracted so strongly, that she might make a mistake. He might be interested, but was it just physical attraction, or could there be more to it?

When she sat down, Hayden moved to the desk and unlocked it. He took out a bag and placed it on the desk. "There's an envelope with your name on it. I had one, too. Mine had a note and two hundred-fifty-thousand dollars in it. Here is yours. I saw your money, but I didn't read the note."

Ginny's eyes widened. Austin had that much money? She took the envelope and opened it. She quickly counted the money and pushed it back in the envelope. She'd give every dime back if Austin was still here. He was strident in his ways, but he was her friend. With trembling fingers, she removed the single folded sheet. With eyes that threatened to spill over with tears, she read,

Ginny, I hope you like the man who will be taking over the ranch. He's a good man. Give him a chance. I am so proud of the woman you've become and want to thank you for all you've done for me these last years.

Austin

She stared at the words and took a deep breath. She had spent eight years working fourteen hours a day. She'd done the books, cooked and tended the horses. Why couldn't he have said something more personal?

"Are you okay?"

Hayden's question brought her out of her daze. "I'm fine." Handing the envelope back to him, she stood. "Could you keep this locked in the desk. I have nowhere safe to put it."

"All right. I'll go into town tomorrow and see about getting a safe for the office."

"You'll have to go to Cheyenne for that. Better to hit the internet. They're faster."

"Sounds like a plan."

She speared him with a glance that demanded the truth. "Hayden, how well did you know Austin?"

"I didn't even know he existed until the lawyer contacted me. I never once met him or spoke to him. I don't know how he even knew about me."

"He showed me pictures, military ones, and talked about all your accomplishments."

"I'm not lying, Ginny. We'll have to go through all the files and see if he had a PI on me."

"I'm going to bed."

Hayden looked piqued. "Did he tell you what you wanted to hear?"

Ginny sucked in a quick breath. His barb had hit home. She was angry that he knew how Austin had let her down. "How dare you? My mail is private. You might like to share what he said to you, but I am more reserved than that." She jerked up from her seat and strode to the door. "Hayden, we've got live and work with each other, but we don't have to be in each other's pockets. Good night."

She made it to her room before the tears fell. Once the dam broke, she cried for hours. There were so many things she cried for, but mostly because Austin had not taken his last chance to tell her he loved her. Yes, he was proud of her but even that had a caveat. *For a woman.* It had been unspoken but there, nonetheless. Exhausted after the emotional upheaval, she fell asleep.

****

The next morning Hayden showered and dressed, then headed for the kitchen. The food didn't smell burned so Ginny must have cooled down. He had known there'd be a fight last night. Ginny loved Austin and felt he'd betrayed her. Some of the blame for the argument was his fault.

He should have kept his mouth shut about the money. He thought she'd feel better knowing the ranch was out of trouble. Somehow, he had to make her understand, the finances were no longer her worry.

As he rounded the corner, he took in the scene. Ryan, Jeff and Mustang Joe were seated at the table, quietly munching on bacon biscuits. The atmosphere ranked close to Los Angeles smog; thick and filled with the smell of trouble. The forecast called for thunderclouds and lots of lightning. Ginny stood at the stove stirring something that smelled like oatmeal.

"Good morning," he said to the men as he poured a cup of coffee. He took a long swallow before turning toward the stove. "Good morning, Ginny."

Her back stiffened and she mumbled a greeting. Still, she didn't turn around.

He sat at the table and placed two biscuits on his plate. Ryan's eyes widened, alerting Hayden that she'd turned. So, he and she had a few words. What was the big deal?

She sat at the opposite end of the table and bent her head as she ate.

"Ginny, you can take the day to run errands," Hayden said.

She looked up and his heart nearly stopped beating. Her eyes were swollen, and dark circles shadowed them. The biscuit in his hand crumbled at the pressure from his hands. "Are you—?"

"I'm fine." She took a biscuit and once more hung her head. "Thank you for the day for errands. The supplies are getting low. What kind of feed will we need for the stud for when he arrives? I can pick it up in town." Her eyes dared him to say anything about her appearance.

Hayden swallowed the last bite of biscuit. "I'll show you the brand after breakfast. Monte will bring some feed, but I'd like to have our own supply. We'll lock it in the storeroom to keep it safe."

Mustang cleared his throat. "The boys have told me about the poisoned horse. I can help keep watch. The reason I came today though, is to tell you I've found the herd's tracks. They're on the Northeast corner of the property by the creek. We'll need to round them up soon before they go higher into the mountains. It's a fine herd.

They'll be perfect for your breeding program.

"Good, we can discuss that after breakfast. Jeff, you and Ryan will be feeding and exercising the horses. No training today."

"Right, boss."

After the two men left the table, Hayden said, "Mustang, I have a little job for you. I'd like you to try and find tracks from our intruder. He must have been watching the place to know when and how to get to the feed."

Mustang scratched his chin. "He is probably someplace high with decent field glasses."

Hayden stood. "I have the right surveillance equipment. You interested?"

"Okay. I'll look for tracks this morning and come back this afternoon dressed appropriately for a night op." Mustang stood and followed the other two out the door. Ginny got up and began clearing the table.

"Leave that," Hayden said. "You can get an early start into town."

She gave him a hard look and though she said nothing, he counted himself lucky he still had his head. Minutes later, he handed her the keys to the old ranch truck. She took them without a word and churned up a cloud of dust as she left. Hayden went inside and saw the dishes. Without a pause, he rolled up the sleeves of his shirt and began washing.

"Excuse me, señor. I'm looking for Miss Ginny. I have an appointment for nine," a young girl said from the doorway.

Hayden cursed beneath his breath. So, this was his punishment. She knew the two women, applicants for part-time help, would be coming this morning.

Remembering his manners, he said, "Ginny had to leave. I'll do the interviews today."

He took in the appearance of the twenty-something young woman. Short and slim with long black hair in a braid. He poured two cups of coffee and motioned for her to sit at the table. "My name is Hayden. I'm the owner." He shook her hand. "What's your name and what kind of cooking experience do you have?" He thought that sounded like a good question to ask.

"My name is Noeletta Garcia, and I have six brothers and sisters. Mama works, so I cook for everyone. My father can no longer do the work he used to, so I need to find work to help out the family."

Hayden saw the need and a little fear in her eyes. This kid needed work and was willing to come out into the boonies to do it. In his previous work, he'd had to make quick judgments about people. Some of those decisions saved his life. He'd trust his gut about the integrity of this young woman.

"You'd be responsible for cooking the mid-day meal and supper. The kitchen, living room, and bath would need to be cleaned. How many days a week can you work?"

"Only four days, señor. I must take my father for treatments on Fridays.

"Could I see your driver's license and social security card?" He hated to stereotype, but her accent and appearance required him to be diligent.

"It is here." The young woman unzipped her little clutch and removed her wallet. In seconds she handed him the credentials he'd asked for.

He pulled out his pen and wrote her information down. He had no idea if the documents were real or forged. What he counted on was a strong work ethic. "Okay. You're hired if you have reliable transportation and show up on time. We eat simply. Ginny will let you know about the rest. Can you start today?"

A look of surprise followed by relief crossed the girl's face. Smiling, she answered, "Yes. What would you like for this meal?"

"Let's start with sandwiches. Just make them big and plentiful. The men work up quite an appetite. "There are four of us and soon there will be more. Afterward, you can set supper up in the crock pot or air fryer. There should be plenty of meat in the freezer.

"Yes, señor."

He was beginning to feel good about his handiwork when another knock sounded on the door. Another woman, older this time, came in. He went back to the coffee pot and poured two more cups of coffee. Two hours later, Hayden made it to the barn. He had hired both women. Noeletta would be the main cook and Janice Reed would work on Friday and Saturday. She'd also cover for Noeletta when needed.

Both women were happy with the arrangement. Lunch had been a success with lots of questions from the men for Noel. She had insisted on the shortened name for convenience.

Chapter Eight

Hayden made his way around the two construction trucks and moved to the new stud barn. The stalls were already in, and the workmen were finishing the tack and storerooms. A few more hours and they would be ready for Salvadore, the stud he was pinning his entire breeding program on. He walked through the structure, checking each section for the horses he hoped to house. Stallions could do a lot of damage to themselves if the surrounding structures weren't strong. He tested the strength of the six-inch studs. "Yep." They were solid."

"Hey, boss?" Ryan called out. "Could you come check this out?"

Hayden moved into the arena where Rebecca stood hitched by a rope to the fence rail.

"Is she all, right?" Ryan asked.

Hayden quickly ran his hand down the horse's belly. Though they were faint, he felt what could be tiny contractions. It was far too early. "Get the vet here as soon as she can make it. It's too early for contractions. Maybe they are what humans call Braxton Hicks."

He moved to her head and looked at her eyes which looked a little glassy. "Hell," he cursed. What did he know? He was a novice when dealing with equine illnesses. Of all times for Ginny to be gone. He couldn't risk Rebecca.

He yanked out his cell phone and speed dialed her

number. She answered on the third ring. He heard music and glasses clanging in the background. She must be having lunch at Jake's bar.

As soon as she answered, he spit it out. "Ginny, it's Rebecca." He heard her swift intake of breath. "We've called the vet, but she needs your special touch."

"I'm on my way. Don't let her die."

His gut clenched when the phone went dead. This horse meant so much to her. He couldn't bear to think of something alarming her. And the foal—God, she could lose the foal. Hayden turned back to the horse. "You're going to be fine," he whispered rubbing a hand across her neck. His hand came away wet. "Damn." This couldn't be good. "Ryan, how hard did you ride her?"

"I just took her around the paddock. She slowed down a lot and I finally brought her in to check her out. She seemed okay or I wouldn't have taken her for exercise."

"I'm not blaming you. I'm just trying to figure things out. She's sweating and it's nowhere hot enough for her to do that. Where are the towels? I'll wipe her down with cool, wet cloths. See if you can get her to drink."

Car doors slammed and both Ginny and Edith Sanderson appeared by Rebecca's side. Hayden stood back and watched helplessly as the vet listened to the horse's heart, then checked her eyes. "Did you check her food trough?" Edith asked Ryan.

"Yes, ma'am. She ate fine this morning and there was no sign of BB's in her food."

Edith ran her hands down Rebecca's belly and frowned. She slid the stethoscope around, listening to different parts. "Unfortunately, there are numerous things a horse can ingest that can be poisonous."

"Shh, you're okay." Ginny rubbed the velvety nose and looked worried. "Is she having contractions?"

Hayden could no longer wait for information. He remembered the conversation with Ginny about becoming too fond of ranch animals. They both had broken the rule. Without speaking, Edith went to her truck and brought back a handheld ultrasound machine. Within seconds, sounds of a beating heart gave all of them hope.

"She's not having contractions. Those are muscle spasms." She took the horse's temperature and cursed. "Dammit to hell. She's got a high fever. You say she was fine this morning?"

"I always check every horse," Ginny said. She was having no problems this morning." Ginny looked to Ryan. "When did you notice anything wrong?"

"When I took her out for her exercise. She was fine at first and then she started slowing down—sluggish-like. I brought her in to check her out."

Edith turned to Hayden. "I think she's ingested some sort of poison. Most likely it's a plant growing natural to this area, and she ate it. Most horses know enough to leave poisonous plants alone but sometimes they get bored and eat them. It will take blood work to figure this out. We don't have the time to wait for results. I'm going to treat her without knowing the toxin. I can't rule out Hemlock or Night Shade. And then there are the fungi spores. The culprit is difficult to determine."

"Will she make it?" His words coincided with Ginny's.

"Will the foal be, okay?" Ginny asked.

"To be truthful, I can't say. I'll treat her with antibiotics, pain reliever and fluids. If she didn't ingest too much, she might be okay. I'm worried about the baby, though. When animals are stressed, nature chooses to fight for the mom."

Hayden swiveled to look at Ginny. Her face was pinched, and her eyes had already started leaking tears. As heartsick as he felt, she looked devastated. He moved to Rebecca's head, petted her by her forelock, and whispered, "You've got to be strong and fight this. I'm counting on you." He wasn't sure if he was talking to Ginny or the horse.

"I'll get my things from the truck. I'll be here the whole time." Edith left the barn.

"Ginny, have you got this?" Hayden asked. "I need to run to town."

"Now?" She asked in disbelief. "Surely, whatever it is can wait. We're in crisis mode."

"It's pretty important. I'll be back in less than an hour. I need to hurry before we lose the light."

"I'm not leaving her."

Her voice told him she disapproved of his leaving. She was vulnerable, caught up in the angst of possibly losing Rebecca or the foal. He couldn't worry about it right now. He was tired of someone messing with his property. This time next week, it could be the two-hundred-fifty-thousand-dollar horse and all his hopes and dreams. He had to find a way to protect Austin's ranch. Hopefully there was a place in town that sold security cams. If not, he'd damn well order them in bulk from the Internet.,

For tonight, he wanted to see who was causing all this mess.

Chapter Nine

Ginny watched Hayden leave. His presence had comforted her. Now, she felt the bitterness of being alone. Others were around her, but she felt isolated—cocooned in a tight shroud of hurt. It had been like this with Austin. How would she handle one more loss?

Would the culprit responsible for this continue to plague the ranch until they went broke? She had no idea how Hayden spent the money. She didn't have access to the books anymore. Hayden kept that to himself just as he did so many things. Was he trying to block her from helping to run the ranch? How could she—?

"Ginny." Ryan shook her. "Come sit down. You're white as a sheet."

His words penetrated her fog and she realized she was shaking. Allowing herself to be led to the bale of hay, she concentrated on putting one foot in front of the other. Ryan helped her to sit, while Jeff brought a cup of water.

Edith paused in her ministrations of the horse to yell over her shoulder, "Put her head between her knees and stand back. She'll be okay in a minute."

Ginny followed the directions and the world stopped spinning and she felt less queasy. The coldness began to recede and she became more aware of her surroundings. Damn, she'd almost swooned. What would the men think? She couldn't show weakness to them. Slowly, she sat up and took a deep breath.

"I'll take that water now, Jeff." She stiffened her spine and sat up ruler straight. "How's she doing, Edith?"

"The same. We need to move her someplace away from the other mares. If she has something contagious, the others might catch it.

Ginny thought for a moment. The new stud barn came to mind but poofed out of existence as a picture of Hayden entered her thoughts. He'd kill her if she contaminated his new barn. "We have an isolation stall on the far side of the barn."

Edith pounced on the idea. "That's perfect. I'll help you move her. It's got to be slow and easy. In the meantime, I need someone searching the paddock for anything out of place."

Ginny threw orders over her shoulder as she gently led Rebecca to the far side of the barn. "Ryan, check the fields. Jeff, get over to the isolation stall and put down hay and water."

Edith ran a hand along the mare's back. "She's sweating profusely now. As soon as she's in the stall we'll get some water down her."

Jeff met them at the stall which was clean and ready. "Should I bring your equipment over, Doc Edith?"

"Yes. And bring a tub of cool water and towels," Edith said. "We need to get her temperature down."

Ginny took the towel from Rebecca's back and wiped at the drool on the horse's muzzle. She was losing fluids fast.

Edith pulled a funnel and hose from her bag. "After I get this down her throat, pour water from the bucket down the tube. Watch it. She might vomit it up—which wouldn't be a bad thing. If she gets rid of the substance in her stomach, she might fare better."

As directed, Ginny poured the water slowly down the funnel into the tube. The horse balked and kicked but the others held her still. She struggled to keep the water from spilling but was only partially successful.

Edith removed the tube and hung it over the side rail. Next, she took out a syringe, filled it with the correct amount of medication and injected the mare. "That should help with the fever and some of the pain. Unfortunately, plant poisoning can be very painful."

Ginny continued to apply wet towels to the horse's body. Suddenly she felt Rebecca tense and strain. "What's wrong?" she asked Edith.

The vet's face tightened and became grim. "She's going into labor. I'll try to stop it with medication, but it might be too late." Once more she pulled out a syringe and a tiny bottle of medicine. She gave the horse the shot and stood back. "I've done all I can. It's up to Rebecca to fight to live."

Ginny placed her forehead against the horse's face. "Come on, Rebecca. I'm right here. Fight, baby." She ran her hand down the mare's belly and prayed the medicine would work.

Rebecca whinnied once, gave a shudder, and delivered the premature foal.

Exquisite pain ripped through Ginny's chest. Tears poured down her face. She hadn't realized how much she had cared for the unborn baby. But she couldn't stop praying yet. Rebecca wasn't out of the woods. From behind her someone slipped the three-legged stool beneath the back of her knees and pushed down on her shoulders. She sat, hard enough to snap her jaw. Her fingers caressed the silky nose of the horse as she whispered encouragement. She could not lose both mother and foal. Numbing hours passed as she sat in front of the horse murmuring words of encouragement. Her voice became raspy as her mind continued to spin. Lord, please let Rebecca live. She wasn't one to bargain but she felt the urge to do so now.

"I think she's over the worst of it. Ginny, you need to take a break."

Edith's voice barely penetrated her fugue state. "What?" Hope bloomed and her heart accelerated. "Is she going to be, okay?"

"I can't promise a hundred percent, but I think she'll make it. I've got my bedroll in the truck. I'll have a snack and then lie down. I'll stay with her all night. You need to rest."

"No. I'll watch her while you sleep." She shifted on the stool and felt a sharp pain race the length of her leg. She needed to move. Her knees wobbled when she stood but she shook off the strong arm that tried to support her.

Turning her head, she saw the owner of the arm. "You're back," she croaked.

Hayden hovered beside her. "I've been here for a while. Ryan is sleeping in the barn in case Edith needs help. You're going to bed."

"I can't sleep until I know one way or the other."

"If Edith says she'll probably be fine, trust her. We'll need your help tomorrow."

They entered the house. The smell of fresh coffee did it. She was ready to refuse again when the aroma wafted to her nose. Making a beeline for the pot, she poured herself a cup.

"Are you sure you want coffee this late?" he asked. "You only have a few hours to sleep."

"Coffee relaxes me. I won't sleep. I'm too keyed up."

Hayden stood, looking uncomfortable. "Ginny, I… You were wonderful with the mare. I'm lucky to have you here. Thanks."

The words may have been halting, but she felt the sincerity in them. "This is my home. There's nowhere else I'd rather be." She picked up her coffee and walked toward her room.

****

Hayden poured himself a cup of coffee, then filled a thermos, feeling that Ryan and Edith might like a cup. Checking the fridge, he smiled. Noel had left a plate of sandwiches. He found a plate, stacked three of the sandwiches on it, and grabbed the thermos. On the way out the door, lights on the road alerted him to the deputy who was supposed to be here hours ago.

The patrol car pulled in beside his truck. The deputy who got out was tall and young. His once crisp uniform now looked tired. "Good evening, Mr. Wilcoyt. Sorry I took so long. We had an interstate pile-up and had to work it first."

Hayden walked toward the barn as he talked. "I understand, deputy—

"My name is Joseph Barns, sir.

"This isn't exactly a smoking gun type of occurrence, but it is a second attempt to kill my horse. I'd like to know if you can do anything about it." He handed the sandwiches to Ryan who stood in the doorway.

"I'm afraid not much," Barns said. "Without proof or a witness, we can only take your statement into evidence. If we should find the guy, it will help prosecute him."

Hayden thought of the statement he'd like to give but

refrained from uttering it. "Do you want to talk to the vet? She's in the barn."

The young officer looked hopeful. "Is Ginny around?"

Hayden didn't like the way everyone seemed to be after Ginny. He chose his words carefully. "I just put her to bed. She was exhausted."

A frown marred the pretty face and Hayden felt a surge of satisfaction.

The young man recovered quickly. "I'll speak to the vet. If she thinks it was poison, that could go a long way to helping to solve the case. Poisons can be traced."

Hayden grimaced but said nothing. Leave it to Edith to burst the man's sleuthing bubble. He followed the deputy into the barn, hoping to rescue his sandwich only to see Ryan scarfing down the last bite.

Deputy Barns was in earnest conversation with Edith, so he walked over to Ryan. "Any change?"

"None, though the vet thinks stable is good. Rebecca's not nearly as calm without Ginny but she needs to rest."

Something in Ryan's voice piqued his interest. "Sounds like you have something to say. Spit it out."

Ryan rubbed his chin. "She'll kill me if she knows I said something."

Hayden was instantly alert. "I'll deal with any attempts at murder. What is up?"

"Ginny nearly fainted this afternoon. Right after you left. She turned ashy colored and was shaking all over. Edith told her to sit with her head between her knees and we gave her some water."

"Is that it?"

"She got all embarrassed and started sending us on

errands."

"Thanks, Ryan." Hayden stood and picked up the now empty plate. He was just in time to walk the deputy out. As the red taillights disappeared through the gate, he wearily made his way into the house.

He had both boots off when he heard it. A mewling sound like a kitten. He got up and checked the kitchen door. There were bound to be a few stray cats around a ranch this size. Finding nothing he moved toward the hall. It was louder now and coming from Ginny's room. She was crying. His gut clenched. He was a sucker for tears.

Easing her door open he peeked inside. "Ginny, are you okay?" His only answer was louder mewling. "I'm coming in."

He received no answer, so he slowly walked in. She lay half covered in the middle of the bed. Her shorty pajamas gave him an eye-opening look at her long legs. Ignoring the jump in his pulse, he sat on the edge of the bed. The light from the hallway illuminated her tear-stained face. Her eyes were closed, and she began to toss the covers about. He shook her gently, to no avail.

"Ginny, wake up. You're having a nightmare.

Her eyes flew open.

It hurt his heart to see the anguish on her ravaged face. Leaning forward he wiped at the tears running down her cheeks. "Shh, it's okay."

She slapped at his hands and cried louder. In between sobs she got out, "What the hell are you doing in my room?"

"I heard you crying and came to check on you."

"I'm…okay."

If only he believed her. Ryan had seen what he

hadn't. "The hell you are. You've been working round the clock, worrying about the horses."

"Is Rebecca all right? I need to go check on her."

"She's fine. I've just seen her, and Ryan and Edith have things under control. You need to get some sleep."

She began to sob in earnest. Her body shook with the intensity of her cries. "The baby died. I couldn't stop it."

Hayden squeezed in beside her and leaned back against the headboard. Wrapping her in his arms, he lifted her onto his chest. She was so distraught she didn't balk at the liberties he was taking. He planted a kiss on the top of her head and let her cry. He didn't know what to say to help her through this. It was like his dad trying to tell him that his dog died. There was no easy way. Ginny would have to live through this and get on with her life. Her sobs wracked her body against his chest. He made soothing noises and gently rocked her. Eventually she calmed to only a few sniffles and a hiccup.

"Are you better now?" Hayden asked.

"I can't cry anymore if that's what you mean."

"I think your body is telling you, you've talked too much tonight."

She leaned in closer. "My body is telling me something a whole lot more important than that. Hayden, I need someone tonight."

Her words brought vivid images to his mind and sent a jolt to his body. He could almost taste her skin; the images were so clear. "It wouldn't be right." He shifted, trying to put a little space between them. "You're vulnerable. I won't take advantage of you."

She leaned in and touched her lips to his. "Who are you trying to convince? I know what I want."

His pulse jerked and he hardened. Damn. How was he going to turn her down without hurting her more? When her fingers began an exploration of his chest, he grabbed her arm and held it with his. "Ginny," his voice deepened, "You've got to listen, honey. You're not thinking straight. If you were yourself, you'd have already had my head for coming in here."

Her body jerked away from him. "Don't tell me what I'm thinking or not thinking. You're the boss but you don't get that power. Kiss me." She waited a heartbeat and said, "Please?"

He knew it was wrong, but he couldn't refuse. Something in her face made him understand how tightly she was wound. He leaned in and pressed his lips against hers. Instantly, his control slipped a notch. When her tongue probed tentatively, he nearly lost it. He opened for her and let her explore. Fireworks exploded in his mind as she continued her search. Dear God, she was sweet.

She pulled back and looked at him in the faint light.

He placed his hand against her cheek, caressing, comforting.

She moved her mouth to kiss his palm. Once more she stared into his eyes. "I need you, Hayden."

The words touched something deep inside him and he wanted her as if his life depended on it. In answer to her plea, he pulled her close against his chest and deepened the kiss. His hand found the swell of her breast beneath the soft tank top. She molded herself to him, bringing his hardness against her belly. He swallowed the moan that escaped her lips with his mouth.

He felt his control slipping. As much as he'd like to devour her, things were getting out of hand. Years of honed life-saving skills alerted him. Something was wrong. He jerked his head up and listened. Someone was in the house.

"What—

"Shh, someone's in the house," he whispered.

She froze.

He gently set her aside and rose. His bare feet gave him an advantage. They wouldn't hear him coming. He entered the hallway, cursing himself for leaving the door open. Sounds of their lovemaking would have carried to the front of the house. It was a good thing his Sig Sauer was in his room. He would likely kill the person who had interrupted. Closing the bedroom door, he silently made his way to the front. He heard the refrigerator slam shut and footsteps. He peeked around the corner and saw Jeff, plate in hand, heading for the table.

Stepping forward, Hayden waited until the plate was safely on the table before speaking. "What the hell are you doing in here?"

"Sorry, boss. Didn't mean to interrupt. I thought I'd get a snack and relieve Ryan," Jeff said, snide clear in his tone.

Hayden thought of what the jerk was implying and wanted to smash his face in. He didn't want rumors to touch Ginny. "This is not your home, Jeff. You have snacks provided in the bunkhouse. You can't just waltz in here any time you feel like it. From now on, only come in the house for meals unless you're sent here for a reason."

"We've always come and gone without a problem."

Taking a sharp breath, Hayden gave Jeff his hardest look. "Now, it's a problem. The old way of doing things won't be in effect anymore. Take your sandwich and go relieve Ryan."

Jeff picked up the plate and headed out the door.

Hayden stifled the urge to lock the door behind him. He wasn't sure the door even had a lock. No one around here seemed to use locks.

****

"Is he gone?"

"Yes. You can go back to bed."

She walked into the kitchen, fully dressed. "I can't go back to sleep and risk another nightmare."

She opened the door, headed for the barn. Anxiety over Rebecca had her feet moving fast over the dusty ground. Her limbs were achy without sleep. She murmured good morning to the barn in general as she made her way to the stall. "What's the verdict?" she asked the vet while settling onto the stool.

"I can safely say she is going to be okay. Whether there are long term problems we'll have to wait and see. Horses who survive poisoning sometimes have lung problems afterward." Edith got up from her sleeping bag and listened to the horse's lungs and belly. "She threw up during the night which made things better for her. Since she's not a racehorse or jumper, she should still be fine for breeding."

"Good," Hayden said behind her.

She hadn't realized he'd followed her from the house. She smelled the soap he'd used, reminding her that she'd skipped her own shower. She didn't look back. She wasn't ready to look him in the eye. She'd thrown herself at the man. He must think her a wanton. Or worse. He was used to girls throwing themselves at him. She didn't particularly care for being one of a crowd.

"What do you suggest for her regimen the next few

days?" Hayden asked the vet.

"If the pasture is clear of whatever plant caused this, let her out in the pasture for two hours, but supervised.

"Ryan found nothing," Ginny said.

"I didn't think he would. Someone must have deliberately thrown the poison in some form over the fence." Edith stood and gathered her things. "I've got clinic this morning, so I need to get back."

"We appreciate all you've done, Edith." Hayden picked up her bag and a few pieces of loose equipment then walked her out to her truck.

Ginny patted Rebecca on the nose and opened the gate. Grabbing her by her halter, she led the horse out to the pasture. She slipped the rope off, then patted the mare on the rump. She climbed onto the fence and sat watching Rebecca nose the grass. They'd had a close call last night. Her mind flashed to what happened between her and Hayden. That had been close too. Dammed if she knew what bothered her more—not having sex with him or how boldly she'd behaved.

She saw Hayden pull out his cell and move from the shadows into the barn. From what she could hear of the conversation; he was calling in a few favors. She didn't like the idea of strangers at the ranch, but they could really use some help. Anyone who came would have to learn fast. When she heard him mention the mustangs, her interest picked up. Her uncle had said they'd only be around for a few more weeks. If the herd made it back up to the mountains, no one would be able to catch them.

Hayden put his phone away and came to stand beside her at the fence. "I have a few friends arriving tomorrow. What's the condition of the bunkhouse?"

"There are three unused bedrooms. I'll go over this

afternoon and give it a brush through and leave clean linens."

"Jeff can do that," Hayden said. "He should be keeping the place clean anyway."

"Guys don't always have the same idea about cleaning as women."

"Tell him to expect an inspection after supper."

Ginny turned to face him. "That's not fair. When will he have time to clean?"

"Give him an hour from his duties. Make it clear that he needs to keep it clean from now on. He tightens up or I replace him."

Ginny worried her lower lip. She wasn't exactly Jeff's biggest fan, but she didn't want to see him fired either.

"This is nonnegotiable."

She balked at his bossy attitude but had little energy to fight him on this. She'd have to pick her fights if she was going to get anywhere with him. "I understand."

His gaze caught hers and held. There was none of the smoky heat she'd seen in his eyes a few hours ago. All she saw was command. She bristled. Her lips were forming her retort to his look when his phone rang. The tension broke and he looked away. Rather than have him breathing down her neck, she went to find Jeff and get it over with. Four steps from the fence and she remembered Rebecca. How could she let her anger at Hayden make her forget her duties? She climbed back onto the fence.

Hayden finished his call and turned back to look at her. The heat was gone, and he smiled. "I can watch Rebecca while I wait on a few more calls. You go do what you need to do."

"Thanks, she mumbled and turned quickly. She still

wasn't ready to look him in the eye and then there were the unneeded words she'd probably say. All in all, she learned something from last night and this morning. Hayden was passionate about everything he did. She'd just bet he'd put as much thought and feeling into oiling the saddles as he did when grooming a horse. Now, how would he treat a woman when he made love? She felt her face burn and desperately looked for Jeff.

She found him in the mares' stables actually doing his job. She watched him a few minutes to make sure he wasn't pretending. He'd been known to dawdle, doing nothing until someone walked in. "Good morning," she said briskly. "Great news about Rebecca."

He stopped and leaned on the rake. "So. she's really, okay?"

"I just got the final word from Edith before she left. She's to be supervised out in the paddock two hours each day. Hayden's doing that now. How many more stalls do you have?"

"Only one."

"Good. Finish that stall and then go clean the bunkhouse. We have three guests coming tomorrow."

His look turned surly. "That's for the cleaning lady. I work with horses."

Ginny wiped her sweaty palms on her jeans. "You have one hour off the clock to get it cleaned. This is to be your job from now on."

"Why doesn't Ryan have to do cleaning?"

Ginny stood a little straighter. "Ryan doesn't get free rent and all his meals here. You can skip the cleaning and pack your things if you'd rather."

"I don't believe you," he sneered. "You need me around here too much."

"Don't count on it. Hayden will inspect the place after supper."

As she turned, her arm was jerked from behind. "Just wait one minute, Miss Tight Ass. No one speaks to me like that and dismisses me like a servant."

"Get your hands off me."

"Don't forget, I heard you and the boss burning up the sheets last night. Fire me and I'll spread the news all over town."

Shock held her still as he spit the words at her. Just what she'd hoped wouldn't happen. Before she could say another word a dangerously low voice interrupted. "The lady said to remove your hands. I suggest you do so, or I'll break them."

Jeff jumped back from Ginny as if burned.

"Ginny, I need you to look out for Rebecca. Jeff and I have a little errand to take care of.

"But—"

"No buts. Just do it."

She had to bite down hard on her tongue to keep from objecting. Hayden was a trained fighter and could do serious harm to Jeff. She was worried.

"I'm not going to break him, though he deserves it. No man can lay a hand on a woman like that in my sight."

"Thanks." Once more, she could only come up with one word.

This time the word held a lot more meaning.

****

Hayden waited patiently for Ginny to leave the barn. He'd nearly grabbed the punk and beat him to a pulp. That anyone would treat her so crassly was unacceptable. He'd not only learned to fight as a SEAL, but he'd also learned patience and restraint and used both now.

"Go to the bunkhouse and clean it. Then pack your bags and leave."

"Why should I bother to clean it if you're going to sack me?"

"Because when you do, you can stop and pickup your pay. No cleaning—no pay."

"You can't do that." Jeff yelled. "I meant what I said about the rumors I'll start."

"I can't stop you from running your mouth, but I also can pass the word about how poorly you worked while here. My suggestion is to leave town and get a fresh start. This all could turn around and bite you in the ass if you're not careful. Think this time before you say or do anything."

Moments later, Hayden heard the bunkhouse door slam. He left the barn and found Ginny walking Rebecca slowly around the pasture. "How's she doing?"

"Just fine. I'll give her a good brush down before putting her away."

"Ginny?"

She turned to look up at him.

"I'm proud of you. You told him what to do in a calm voice and followed through when he didn't comply. Never let another man treat you like less than what you are."

"If I'd had grit, I'd have done it long before now."

"You were treated like a lesser person and that causes you to second guess yourself. Who did it to you?"

"What? "Her voice raised two notches and cracked.

Hayden watched the fear and doubt negate his previous words of praise. "Who took your self-confidence away? Was it Austin?"

"No! He treated me with respect even if his ways

were a little outdated. He was always a gentleman."

"Who then?" he persisted.

"I'm not ready to talk about it."

"When will you be ready?"

"It's not that I don't trust you…I…can't. I'm sure I should get counseling, but I can't bring myself to do it. I couldn't talk about it to a stranger."

"Do you still think of me as a stranger?" He waited. After last night he couldn't believe she still shied from personal conversation with him. Dammit they'd almost been lovers. Surely that had to count for something.

"Not a stranger, but not my best friend either. Some things take time, Hayden. I have lots of bars up around that part of my life."

"I can wait, but Jeff will still blab and embellish what he heard last night. Can you live with that? Will it bother you to have people believe we're lovers?" He waited several minutes for her answer.

"Only if it wasn't true."

Her words sucked the breath from his lungs. So last night hadn't been a minute of pain induced need. She really wanted him. "Is that an invitation?"

"Hayden?"

"What?"

"You talk too much."

Her arms reached up and wound around his neck. His heart pounded with anticipation as her lips found and opened over his. Damn, she tasted good. His hands pulled her in, molding her to his body. A loud clanking jerked him back. He set her away from him as Ryan came from the barn.

"I can put Rebecca back in her stall."

Hayden sent him a look of appreciation for his tact.

"Good. Things are going to be busy in the next few days. I fired Jeff and I have three friends coming to help us until we can get things worked out."

Ryan took the halter from Ginny. "I'm not surprised about Jeff. He has too much arrogance for a job like this. Besides, it was just a job to him. He didn't really care about the horses."

"Thanks for doing an excellent job, Ryan. I wish I could find more like you."

"I'll keep my ear to the ground," Ryan said and led Rebecca back to the barn.

"What's left to do?" Hayden asked.

"I need to check on the work horses, then try to get some training in."

"You go train. I'll take care of the animals." Reluctantly he turned and left her standing there.

Chapter Ten

Hayden pushed the stack of bills to the back of the desk before pulling on his boots. With Jeff gone, he'd need to help with the feedings. He could also take a turn with Rebecca and free up Ginny and Ryan to work with other horses. Without needing to train Rebecca for the show, Ryan could work with some of the younger horses. Grabbing another cup of coffee in the kitchen, he got ready to go out.

"Señor? Your friends will be here by lunch time?" Noel handed him a muffin to go with the coffee. Breakfast had been quick this morning as everyone left for the barn early to get a head start.

"Yes. If I know my buddies, they'll be here in an hour or so. Let's plan on a late lunch and a snack in the barn in an hour. These men eat lots of food, so be prepared. Do we have enough supplies, or do we need a grocery run?"

"We have enough for today, but I will need more for the rest of the week."

"Put together a list and one of us will go out later this afternoon." He downed the last of the coffee, set the cup on the table, and left. It was already hot at nine-thirty in the morning. He hated having to do the paperwork first, but it was overdue.

"Morning, boss, "Ryan said as Hayden walked out of the shadows. Ryan was working with Jasmine, a beautiful gray with black points. "We're finished feeding up, so I jumped in on training."

Hayden looked around and spotted Ginny hard at work mucking out stalls. He grabbed a rake and shovel and moved to the cubicle closest to him. He wasn't above shoveling a little manure and straw and found a measure of peace in the mindless physical labor. He thought of the snack he'd ordered for later and thought an outside picnic table would be a welcome addition to the barn. He also had plans to put a bathroom in the old storage room by the tack room. These were things that should have been done years ago.

Austin seemed to have lost all track of the finer amenities to concentrate on just getting by. He couldn't blame him. At his age, he could be forgiven his thoughtlessness. He was sure Ginny had been aware, but she only worried about making ends meet. Once more, he felt a degree of anger for his grandfather for holding on to the money and not keeping the place up. He picked up the handles of the cart and headed for the outside.

Ginny paused in her work and looked out the front. "Hayden. I think your friends are here."

He finished dumping the load and came back inside. "I had a feeling they would show up early. Those guys like to make it in time for all the meals."

After the black SUV pulled to a stop, all the doors opened. He was surprised to see four people get out. He'd only called three. A closer look revealed that Monte had also come with the group. He dusted his hands down his pants and moved forward to greet the men. All were tall and looked as dangerous as he knew them to be. "Ginny, Ryan, come meet my friends."

Monte Larkin moved forward, grasped his hand, and

enveloped him in one of his well-known bear hugs. "Man, I was so disappointed you didn't ask me along."

Hayden had to look up a little to meet his friend's eyes and saw worry in them.

"What's this I hear about horse poisoning and threats?" Monte asked.

"I'll explain only once so, let's get the introductions made." Hayden moved to shake hands and clasp shoulders with the other three men.

"Ginny, Ryan, this is Monte Larkin, my partner, and the steely eyed giant next to him is Adam Nolte." He indicated the next man whose crop of brown hair was just shy of shaggy. "This is Cooper Hayes. Next to him is Peyton Brown. They've always had my back. Gentlemen, meet Ryan my ranch hand and trainer, and Ginny the heart of Wilcoyt ranch."

"Might have known there'd be a beautiful woman involved," Cooper mumbled.

"Mind your manners, gentlemen," Hayden said. "This woman will tear a strip off your hide and leave you in tears before you can wink an eye." He caught sight of Noel coming toward them with a tray laden with food. "Everyman grab a bale of hay and we'll eat our snack outside."

Noel placed the tray on one of the bales and swiftly took her leave.

Everyone dug in and for the next few minutes the friends caught up.

"So, we need to get to the bottom of your troubles before we bring the stallion over," Monte stated.

"Yes," Hayden said. "Plus, I need to round up the wild mustangs while they're in the lowlands. I figure two of you can stay here while Mustang, Ginny and I go catch a few horses. Ryan, will you be able to take care of things with two of these guys for help."

"Sure, boss, but I hate to miss out on the mustangs." Ryan scarfed down another chocolate chip cookie.

"I'll make sure you make the next trip. After the break, show the other three the ropes. I'll show Monte the ranch and the books. When you catch up, show them the bunk house and let them get settled."

He and Monte left the barn and moved toward the stud barn.

"How's the mare that was poisoned?" Monte asked as they walked through the newest addition to the outbuildings.

"She lost her foal but will live. Someone deliberately threw something over the fence for her to eat. Ginny was devastated by it. Austin gave her the mare for a gift and from what I gather, she didn't receive very many gifts."

Monte pushed against some of the stall walls and grunted his approval. "How does she fit into everything?"

"I don't have the whole story, but she ran away from home at fourteen. Austin took her in, and she's been doing everything including the dishes. Her real talent though is horse whispering. I don't claim to understand all the mumbo jumbo, but she has a special way with animals. They'll do anything for her, and she barely needs to touch them."

"The place is a little run down, but it's a sweet property. I thought you had more workers than just the one guy," Monte commented.

"One quit and I fired another yesterday after he put his hands on Ginny."

Monte stopped and gave Hayden a questioning look. "Ouch, is that a keep away signal I hear?"

Hayden removed his hat and wiped his brow on his sleeve. He eyed Monte before speaking. "I'll be the first to admit I want her. I haven't touched her but I'm not sure how long that will last. I don't want her to get hurt. According to the will, she has lifetime use of the ranch, house, and an acre of property. There was also a sum of money. It seems my grandfather didn't let anyone know he had three-hundred-thousand-dollars sitting in a safety deposit box." He pointed out the hay barn and the work-horse stables as they continued their tour. His note to me said he'd been saving for a stallion. Seems he and I had the same dream."

Monte followed Hayden into the house. "Do you have any leads on who might be causing all this?"

"I have a guess. There's a land broker who claims to have a lien on the ranch. I have some lawyers from Cheyenne looking into it. This guy is about as slimy as they get. The hard part will be proving anything. Until I can get some reliable help, I need you guys to make sure everyone is safe. So far, there's been no action against people, but I don't think it'll stay that way."

Monte hung his hat on the rack by the door. "Looks like this place is stuck in the seventies."

Hayden should have felt offended at the comment but instead, he gazed around the room, trying to see it from a stranger's point of view. "Yeah, well, I haven't been here long enough to start redecorating. The place has three small bedrooms. I intend to convert the attic into a master bedroom after things settle. My priority was getting the stable built."

Monte followed Hayden into the kitchen and

grabbed a cup for coffee.

Noel came out of the storeroom and rushed to help with the coffee. "Are all your friends big like this one? I'll have to double the order I had prepared."

Hayden laughed. "You're right. They're all big. It was almost a requirement for my last job." He took his cup and headed for the office.

Monte raised his brow and grinned. "You conduct business out of your bedroom?"

"More like I sleep in my office. It just didn't feel right, sleeping in Austin's room." Hayden moved a stack of books, clearing a chair for Monte to sit. "I'm still going through the books and sorting through bills and paperwork.

Monte frowned. "You can't do it all by yourself. First order of business is to get you some staff. I suggest you not bother with the house. Hire a project manager and have him take over those changes. Have you thought about adding on or just building a new home?"

"I'd like to keep the same house. It feels like the heart of the place. Besides, I'm certain Ginny wouldn't like the idea of a new house. She's had few roots in her life. Austin gave her that. She'll want to keep things the same."

Monte sent Hayden a questioning stare. "Pardon me if I'm wrong, but you seem to place a lot of emphasis on what Ginny wants. Are you sure about your feelings there?"

"No. I'm not sure of anything when it comes to Ginny. I do know that she breathes life into the ranch. Without her it's just a bunch of buildings."

"All right," Monte said with a nod. "Let's see those books."

Chapter Eleven

Supper was a noisy affair. Six men and her, the only female, made things tense. She felt the testosterone in the air and the open attention from two of the men directed toward her.

She watched Hayden frown at Cooper, who had smiled at her and leaned in and murmur something that only she could hear. He was an absolute flirt, but she knew it was all in fun. Hayden, who clearly hadn't gotten the memo, glared fiercely at the man. She stood and picked up her plate. "If you gentlemen will excuse me, I'll leave you to talk without your filters on. I haven't heard a curse word all night. Though I appreciate the gentlemanly behavior, I'm sure you have stories to swap that I don't want to hear. Good night."

A chorus of "good nights" followed her down the hall. She closed her bedroom door and leaned back against it. As tired as she was, she should go straight to sleep but that wasn't going to happen. Going into the bathroom, she cleaned up before changing into her pajamas. Her body was tense and stiff. Using the little lighter by her bed, she lit the scented candle and tried to relax. She couldn't remember the last time she'd felt this jacked up. Images of nature which she tried to conjure were replaced by a face that was achingly familiar. One by one, his features were not arresting, but together they made the lower part of her body tighten. It didn't take a psychic to figure out why she felt tense and needy. Sexual attraction. She was loathe to think how long she'd been without intimacy. Damn—she ached.

The voices from the kitchen let her know that Hayden was enjoying his friends. Irritated, she picked up her phone and pulled up the flute meditation she had saved. Maybe it would drown out the men's laughter. It was too easy to hear Hayden's laughter. She wished he'd do that with her. Soon the delicate notes of the flute caused her to relax, and she drifted off in a restless sleep.

****

Hayden shut the kitchen door and locked it. As much as he enjoyed his friends, he needed some quiet time to unwind. Touring the men around the ranch brought an excitement about building his business. He moved into the office, anxious to start putting his plans on paper. He removed his boots and clothes, leaving on his skivvies. He wasn't sure about the etiquette of doing office work in his briefs but the hell with it. It was his office and his bedroom. He wrote a few ideas and slammed the pen down. It wasn't working.

He'd tried everything to get Ginny out of his head all day. He looked for her around each corner of the barn or arena. What happened last night couldn't just be shoved back into the genie bottle and corked. They'd come within seconds of making love. He hardened at the thought. Dammit, he'd been semi-hard all day. Riding Trigger had been an exercise in pain.

A sound came from down the hall. Instantly, he was alert and moved toward the intermittent sound. The melodious notes of a flute drifted through the door of her bedroom along with the scent of sage and something tangy. The light coming from beneath the door wasn't the overhead, he was sure. It must be a lamp or a candle. He raised a hand to knock on her door. As he did, he caught sight of his briefs. Damn he couldn't talk to her like this. Without another thought he went back to his bedroom and donned his jeans.

What was he thinking? She was probably just meditating and maybe chanting some of her tribal language. He listened, detecting only the slightest sound of the flute. He'd sat up hours with his friends. She should be asleep. It wasn't like the music bothered him. With his door shut he'd barely heard it. Should he go back and knock? If she answered he knew what would happen. Though he wanted it, now wasn't the right time.

A cry came from her room. Not the 'I'm having a bad dream' sort of cry. There was fear in her voice. He sprinted to her door just as she screamed. "No! Leave me alone. Get away!"

He didn't bother to knock and shouldered the door open, and the frame splintered. She was lying on the bed thrashing and kicking. Her words were incoherent now. He sat on the edge of the bed and called her name. "Ginny, wake up. You're having a nightmare."

Hayden felt gut punched at the condition she was in. He had to wake her. He placed a hand on her shoulder, and she threw a punch at his face. She screamed and scratched at him.

"Get away! Don't touch me!"

He dropped his hand and sat back. Her cries evoked something fiercely primitive in him. Something protective. This problem couldn't be solved with fists or guns. Forcing her to be still, wouldn't work. He could hold her without restraining her. Maybe his touch would get through to her. He stood and lifted her from the bed and slid beneath her. Settling her against his chest he let her thrash as he gently spoke soothing words. Slowly, the thrashing stopped, and she began to cry. Her sobs tore at his heart.

"Are you awake now?"

She inhaled deeply and swallowed a cry. "Ye-ess." That single word came out broken and barely above a whisper.

His first instinct was to wrap her in his arms, but the words she had cried stopped him. This must be the secret she wouldn't discuss. After his career ending wounds, he'd spent hours in therapy and found out quickly that it was better to get things out in the open. It was obvious someone had attacked her. He wanted to strangle whoever it was.

"I'm here to listen if you want to talk," he breathed against her ear.

She turned and snuggled against his neck as she inhaled deeply. "Just hold me for a while."

His heart lightened a little. She trusted him. With trust they could work out the rest. Wrapping his arms around her body he pulled her close. He got a look at her face before she hid it against his chest. Tear stained and swollen it made him hurt to know she'd suffered this nightmare. She sniffled and her breath hitched, but he felt her relax against him. Softly, he rubbed her back in a circular motion, trying to ease the tense muscles. She was quiet so long that he thought she'd drifted off. He stopped his rhythmical rubbing and waited.

She turned to face him. "Make love to me, please. I can't stand that memory and I want to wipe it away."

His pulse jerked in reaction. If he made love to her now all kinds of things could happen. She could get frightened and mistake him for her attacker. He could handle that by just backing off and leaving but what if she got all emotionally tangled up. Could he do more harm than good? But she'd said please. How could he not do as she asked? Damn this was a can of worms. He pushed her hair from her covered face. Running a hand down her cheek he watched for any small sign of distress.

"Look at me." The command was gentle yet insistent. She rolled her head until her face was mere inches from his own. Damn, he'd forgotten his own attraction to her. His feelings for her were unsure, but they were there. If they were to make love just to wipe a memory away, where would that leave them.

"Well?" She dragged the word out. Her voice barely above a whisper.

His decision made, he leaned in and kissed her. He didn't pull her closer, allowing her the room to move away if she wanted. The kiss was gentle. His lips brushing against hers. She tasted sweet and vaguely like what he imagined the flavor of shock would be. All salty dampness with undercurrents of sweat and woman.

Nibbling the side of her mouth, he spread butterfly kisses across her cheek. She moaned and he tamped down his urge to ravage her mouth. When she reached for him, he lightly took her hand and kissed her palm, licking her lifeline to her wrist. Her pulse beat rapidly.

She pulled her hand free and cupped his cheek. "Are you always so gentle?"

He chuckled. "Am I doing this wrong?"

She reached in and nipped his lip, then tongued it as if to atone for her transgression. "Don't be afraid to love me, Hayden. I won't break. I may be upset and have bad memories, but I'm not made of crystal. I won't shatter if you handle me."

He studied her eyes to judge her sincerity. "I'm a big man and I don't want to frighten you." He lifted her and rolled her until she straddled him. She'd feel less afraid this way. Her bottom sat deliciously against his erection. He gently ran his hands along her thighs.

****

His response to her touch made her feel powerful. Ginny ran her hands across his chest, teasing the bit of hair she found there. When her fingers touched his nipples, he sucked in a breath. She smiled in satisfaction. Beneath her fingers, his chest muscles bunched. She traced her tongue down the path her fingers had taken He tasted of man, heat, and something uniquely Hayden. She wanted to lap him up like a cat with a bowl of cream. The bulge beneath her bottom grew larger, harder, causing her breath to come in little pants. Pausing in her exploration, she pulled at his shirt, popping buttons in her haste. His abs stood out like ripples along the shore.

He pulled the hem of her shirt over her head. Her breasts peaked proudly before him. Every fiber of her being willed his mouth to touch her. When he complied, she moaned. Pulling his head closer, she ran her fingers through his hair, holding him close. Ginny protested when he moved his head, turning away from her as he stood, quickly shucking his clothes. Her attention was completely caught when she saw him.

His legs were finely muscled, and his manhood jutted proudly. She gazed at his ripped abdomen and hard as steel chest. She'd never been with a man this perfect before. His masculine beauty gave her a moment of pause. What was he thinking about her? She knew she was pretty, but did her body make him feel quivery as his did for her? When she finally looked up, his gaze met hers. He flashed her a wicked grin, and a frisson of electricity jolted her heart. Keeping her eyes pinned on him, she reached into the drawer on the bedside table and pulled out several red foil packets.

His brow shot up and she smiled. "I like to challenge a man," she got out huskily before she blushed.

He moved forward joining his fingers with hers. "I like an ambitious woman."

The move brought his chest even with her mouth. She brushed her tongue across his nipple and smiled against his skin as his whole body went taut. Quickly, he pulled her head up and took her mouth, seared a path over her lips as his tongue delved deeply inside. Coming up for air, he helped her rip off her clothes. He gently pushed her back against the pillows kissing a path down her throat to her breast. He suckled as his hand slid south until he touched her honeyed mound. She tightened around his hand as he found her nub. Finding a rhythm, he moved his finger against her in a circular motion. She gasped, then shuddered as her body exploded in a blast of light and tingles. With deft fingers he had the foil package open and covered himself in protection.

Still reeling from the onslaught of sensations, she groaned in pleasure when he entered her. She caught the rhythm and moved with him. He watched her with penetrating eyes, searching for signs of distress at his possession. When she didn't hesitate, he increased the pace until her mind and body shattered. He groaned and found his own release after hers.

Ginny rolled to her side, watching him beneath the thick tresses covering her cheeks. "Thank you."

Her words slammed into his chest like a bullet into flesh. Why the hell was she thanking him. Hayden sat up. "What the hell do you mean?"

She pulled the sheets up to cover her breasts. "Just what I said. I needed a friend, and you were there."

Hayden quickly pulled on his jeans and stood. His jaw tightened. He'd like to say more but those sheets held tightly against her chest said enough. She may have worked away the demons temporarily, but they were still there. "I'll start breakfast while you shower. The guys will be up early. Most of them like to run five miles before breakfast."

"All right. I have the makings for sausage biscuits in the fridge."

He left her room, collected a shirt, then slid his feet into his boots. He tried to shove what had just happened to the back of his mind. He turned his thoughts instead to the day before him. If he knew Monte, he'd been up for at least an hour.

Moments later there was a tap at the door. He moved to open it and saw Monte and Cooper standing on the porch. He opened the door and pointed the way to the coffee. The men poured mugs and sat at the table. He turned the sausage before acknowledging the 'good morning,' the two grunted between sips.

Monte gave him a look. "You're still dressed in yesterday's clothes. Don't tell me you stayed up all night?"

Hayden laughed. "Hardly, though I did stay up late."

Monte poured a second cup of coffee. "If you were working on the books, you've got to get an accountant. They're worth their weight in gold come tax time."

Cooper moved around the table and opened the

fridge. He pulled out the eggs. "Do you want these scrambled or fried?"

Ginny walked into the kitchen her hair damp from her shower. "We're having sausage biscuits. I have a metal form I put down on the griddle."

"You got this?" Hayden asked. "I'll just take a quick shower."

Cooper answered, "We got it. Who's making the biscuits. I can only do the canned kind."

Ginny pushed him aside and pulled a bag of dough from the fridge. I made the dough last night, so I only have to roll them out."

Monte asked, "What can I do?"

"Empty what's left of the coffee into the carafe. You'll find it just above the pot. Then make another pot. The fixings are by the carafe." Ginny found the egg form and handed it to Cooper. "Be sure and spray it first."

"Yes, ma'am." His deep throated response got a chuckle out of Monte.

"You boy's will have to get used to my bossiness. It's an old habit.

Chapter Twelve

Ginny put the last of the hay into the stall and headed for the feeding station. She motioned for Adam, Cooper and Peyton to join her. Might as well get all trained at once. She figured Monte would be going on the Mustang hunt and was well versed in feeding horses anyhow.

"First, go to the board and choose your horse. They all get feed and fresh water put down each morning and evening. Each horse has a vet approved diet of prescribed food and nutrient supplements. We'll start with Rebecca who is our special case. She's on an easily digested food made to cause as little stomach distress as possible. She was recently poisoned and lost her foal."

"How soon is recently? "Adam asked.

"Two days ago." She heard her voice crack and tightened her grip on the top of a food dispenser. Blinking hard to block tears, she continued "She was fed BBs the first time. The second time, they threw a poisonous plant over the fence. She nearly died and her foal did. The bastards had to choose the only pregnant mare we had."

Cooper reached out and put a hand on her shoulder. "I'm sorry this happened. Now, that we're here, it won't happen to any other horse. The three of us are specialists in security and will keep things safe."

"Got that right," Peyton chimed in.

"Right." Ginny grabbed a bucket. "In addition to her

food, she gets the listed vitamins. I just pour her mixed grains in the bowl, bring the bowl to the vitamin station and add the liquid. Next, cut up an apple or carrot and put it on top. We've been keeping Rebecca inside except for two hours a day. She's the pretty lady in stall six."

All three men turned their gazes to the stall.

Ginny carried the food bucket over and set it in the little box on the rail. Running her hands down Rebecca's neck, she murmured softly to the horse. The horse nickered and head-butted Ginny before sticking her head in the bucket. Hayden and Monte walked in as she was finishing up with Rebecca.

Hayden joined the others outside the stall. "Here's Rebecca, the horse I told you about." He turned to Ginny. "After feeding, could you take Monte and I on a quick tour of the land? He'll see some of it on the Mustang hunt, but I just want to give him a feel for the place."

She looked at the blond-haired bear of a man next to Hayden. She found it so hard to understand how someone who could look so cuddly should have such a violent job. He must have done many violent acts as a Navy SEAL though. As Hayden's partner, she supposed he was her boss, too. He did own half the business after all. The idea still rankled. Worry played at the back of her mind, but she kept her voice neutral. "Of course. Ryan's horse should fit him well. You'll ride Trigger, right?

Loud chuckles spread through the men. "I told you he was a cowboy," Cooper said. More laughter followed his words and Hayden joined in.

Ginny looked around at the men. "If everyone will catch a horse, we can get feeding done quickly. You guys can feed the work horses while we're gone."

"Yes, ma'am," a chorus of male voices said at once.

Monte looked at Hayden and pulled a five dollar bill out and placed it in his hand. "I see what you mean," he said with a grin.

Everyone seemed to get the joke but her. For a moment it hurt, then she stiffened her spine and grabbed a halter. "Follow me."

An hour later the three riders left the barn, heading for the trail used to train the horses.

"Looks like the fields could be planted and reduce feeding costs." Monte said.

"Yeah, I haven't had the time to get to it." Hayden replied.

Ginny led the way down the path. "When Austin got sick, and money got tight it was easier to buy the hay instead."

"How many acres do you have?" Monte asked.

"Around four-thousand," Hayden said. "I haven't seen it all yet, but when we go mustang hunting, we'll see a goodly portion."

Ginny turned left where the path split. "Some of the prettiest areas are where the mustangs summer. They come down from the hills in spring for foaling and spend several weeks fattening up before going back into the hills. We'll have a short window to catch them. Once they get back up to the hills there are too many places to hide."

Hayden followed her through the turn and trotted up beside her on the widened trail. "When I was in town I went to the little museum. Legend says this property is where the second stagecoach robber hid. Any ideas about that?" He waited several minutes and wondered if she would answer.

"Legends usually tend to have a little truth in them. The elders talk of a place on this property. It was supposed to have a dead body on it. No one mentioned where it was. My people are very closed mouthed about things like that. Places where people die frighten them."

Monte pulled in closer. "Sounds like a reason to want the property. Have you had to get rid of treasure hunters?"

"Yes, though not many lately. Usually, the summer is worse."

"Maybe its treasure hunters poisoning the horses," Monte said.

Hayden thought a minute. "That wouldn't make sense. They don't need the property to search for treasure. All they'd have to do is stay out of sight of the ranch hands. The place is big enough to do it."

They came over a rise where the riders stopped and dismounted. The scene warranted it. A small lake with wild grasses and shrubs made it look like an oasis. Two River Birches created shade near the bank. Startled, three wood ducks took to the air in a noisy display.

"This is Teardrop Lake," Ginny informed them.

"Damn, what a nice lake," Monte said. "I wish I had my fishing tackle. This place looks perfect for bream."

Hayden laughed. "I'm afraid those breams are going to have to wait. I'll get some tackle and have it on hand."

"Sounds good," Monte said. "This would be perfect for a little cabin."

"I'm going to put some small cabins in closer to the house. I figured I have a better chance of keeping ranch hands if I have a place for their wives and families. I'll still have the bunk house for bachelors."

Ginny's hands clenched on the reigns. Her chin

tilted up and her jaw clenched. Hayden and Monte were making all these plans, and no one had included her. She had no right to complain but it pissed her off. She'd struggled for years to keep the ranch alive. Surely her thoughts might be useful.

"Do you have any ideas about attracting more employees, Ginny?" Hayden asked.

She relaxed a little and said a mental sorry to him. Maybe he did want to know what she thought. "We could set something up with the university's Veterinarian or Animal Husbandry program. Maybe do an internship with students for a semester. That would give us some extra help during the busy months."

"That's a great idea. We would have a continuing supply of young workers," Hayden said. "We could even offer a scholarship program. I like it."

Ginny remounted. "Just how many are you looking to hire?"

Hayden and Monte mounted their horses and exchanged a look before Hayden answered. "About ten at first. Later we'll fill the more technical jobs by advertising in the equestrian magazines. I figure we'll end up with about thirty people in all."

"You'll need to set up some sort of cafeteria building and add cooks and cleaners," Monte added.

Ginny's eyes widened. "I hadn't realized it would be so big. We need to get back before dark. She galloped off in the lead.

Chapter Twelve

By the time Hayden came into the kitchen, breakfast was ready. "Morning, Ryan," he said as he poured a cup of coffee from the carafe. Adam and Peyton joined them at the table. "Noel asked if her brother and father could help us out here at the ranch. That gives us some extra help."

Peyton grabbed two biscuits before the plate made it to the table. "Where's the tracker? I'm looking forward to meeting a Native American with some of the old skills."

Hayden placed a bowl of sliced oranges and strawberries next to the plate of sausage biscuits. "He's sort of an uncle to Ginny. I've only seen him a few times. He helps out part time, but he chooses the hours."

Cooper laughed. "Nice work if you can get it. Sort of like our old job without the exotic locations."

No one had to be told what job he referred to. Hayden recalled the grueling hours and danger associated with being on the SEAL teams.

At that very moment, the kitchen door opened, and Mustang Joe strode in. Well over six feet, broad shouldered, with two long black braids over his shoulders, the man made a lethal impression. Joe made a beeline for the table and grabbed a plate. Several of the men leaned against the counter as they ate.

"Joe, I brought in a few reinforcements," Hayden

said. "This is Monte, my partner, and retired team members, Peyton, Adam, and Cooper. They are in security now and available to help us. Gentlemen, this is Mustang Joe. I'm told he's the best tracker in the state."

Joe nodded to each of the men, then turned to Hayden. "Are they all going on the hunt?"

"No, just Monte and Peyton. The other two will stay here to guard the place and help Ryan with the chores."

"Has anything bad happened here in the last two days?" Mustang asked.

"Things have been quiet. We're watching the horses like hawks so we may have heard the last of our horse killer." Hayden glanced at Ryan to see if he was spooked by talk of their troubles. So far, he had handled things well but, Ryan had a wife and her welfare had to be in his thoughts. When they had time to build cabins, they would be a Godsend.

Mustang pulled a laminated map from his back pocket. Clearing a spot on the table, he smoothed the folded paper. Running his hand along the map, he pointed out the route they'd take to the creek and the spot where he hoped to find the horses. "With your two men and my three roustabouts, that will give us seven." Joe shrugged. "It should be enough. There's a little gully before we reach the creek. We'll make camp there…"

"There will be eight. Ginny is coming with us," Hayden said in a voice that brooked no opposition.

"But I'll be needed here at the ranch," Ginny said.

"See, I told you she had a thing for me," Cooper said, slapping Adam on the back as the two of them left to start feeding the stock.

Hayden took in her upturned chin, fiery eyes, and muscles quivering with objections. "No."

She took a step closer to him, edging into his personal space. "Don't be so unreasonable."

He dug down deep, searching for a little calm and a lot of patience. "This is the beginning of our new business. I want you there with us."

"Why? It's not like I'm a real part of it anyway. I would do better to train horses. That, I can do."

Hayden saw the hurt in her eyes, but now wasn't the time for explanations. "I want you there to calm the horses. I don't want them stressed in this heat."

Ryan, looking uncomfortable, pushed his chair under the table, and left the two to their discussion.

Thirty seconds later a rifle shot sounded outside. Reaching for the gun he wasn't wearing, Hayden ran for the door but slowed to peek out. Ryan was lying in the sand, blood pouring from his shoulder.

"We've got our guns," Adam yelled from his spot by the barn door. "Stay inside."

"You'll need cover so you can get to Ryan," Hayden said. "Give me two minutes." It took only thirty seconds to grab the Remington from over the fireplace and return. He cracked the door and called out, "On three, get Ryan while I cover you."

"Roger that," Adam and Cade called in unison.

Hayden yanked the door open. "Three." He had no idea where the shooter was, so he fired several rounds into the air.

Adam and Cade ran to where Ryan lay, grabbing him under the arms and rushing him to the barn. Still firing, Hayden followed the men into the barn and closed the door. "Put him on the hay bale."

After the two men helped Ryan sit up, Adam cut the bloody shirt from his wound with his pocketknife.

"It's just a graze," Cooper said over Adam's shoulder. "No slug to worry about."

Ryan yelped at their ministrations. "That's because it's not your arm."

Hayden took in the bloody shirt and Ryan's pale face. This was it. A line drawn in the sand. Whoever the bastard was, he had crossed it. Heat coursed through his veins as anger burned his belly. Dammit to hell, this had to end.

A siren coming down the road drew him up short. He put the rifle down and eased the door open. The shooter was probably long gone so he met the sheriff as he got out of the car.

"What the hell's going on out here?" The sheriff asked. "Horses poisoned, now shots fired. You seem to attract trouble, Wilcoyt."

Hayden sucked in a breath before releasing his pent-up anger on the closest person, Sheriff Jake Bannister.

"I've played by the rules and minded my own. Things keep happening. Now, I have a man shot while he was walking to the barn. I'm mad as hell and don't care who knows. I'm used to taking care of my own problems, but this time I brought in some help. I hired four security specialists who won't be afraid to shoot back."

"How bad?" Bannister demanded.

"There's no slug but it'll need cleaning and stitching."

Bannister grabbed his radio and spoke sharply. "Send an ambulance to Wilcoyt ranch and call in Fred from the Interstate."

Bannister allowed the radio to drop back to his shoulder. He gave Hayden a steely look from eyes nearly obsidian black. With his wide shoulders and height, he looked formidable. "Mr. Wilcoyt, you're new to the ranching business and I'll cut you a little slack, but no one goes around half-cocked, shooting at people. You do have the right to defend your property, and Wyoming is an open carry state, but you better stay within the letter of the law."

When the sheriff finished the calmly delivered speech, Hayden rocked back on his heals. He admired any man, especially a lawman, who knew where he stood and didn't back down.

He grinned and stuck out his hand. "You're right. You have my word we'll stay within the law—while still protecting my own."

After the two shook hands, the atmosphere eased. Everyone moved back into the barn and huddled around Ryan. The wail of the ambulance had them standing back as Hayden and the sheriff went to direct the ambulance crew.

****

Hours later, Ryan had been stitched up, statements had been taken, and everyone returned to their chores.

Hayden was hard at work mucking out stalls. He paused, leaning on the pitchfork to take a breather. Everyone around him had a tightly bound tension about them. Ginny was busy working with a young gray horse with black points. Jasmine was their youngest mare and still had a long way to go until she was ready to breed or sell. Ginny patiently corrected the horse when she made a mistake. The entire time she whispered praise and admiration. The horse eagerly responded. The magic she had with horses was amazing.

Monte called from the barn doors. "Hayden, looks

like the ATV's are here."

"Thanks."

He walked out to where the noisy machines were still running. Both vehicles had wagons hitched to their rears, ready to be filled with supplies. Tents, horse feed, and ropes filled one of the wagons. The other had a portable stove and the food supplies. Hayden looked over everything with a critical eye. When he'd been with the teams, the right equipment meant the difference between life and death. Making sure it was in proper order prior to needing it was crucial. He had a feeling Mustang Joe was just as efficient.

Ginny came from the house and stood next to the wagons. She gazed at the equipment as if looking for faults. "Where's the gasoline?"

Hayden sucked in a breath. He'd missed that.

The roustabout gave Ginny a whiter-than-white smile. "Sam stopped in town to pick it up. He should be here in a few minutes."

As Hayden threw the man a look, his smile faded. It was petty, but he just couldn't stand another man looking at Ginny the same way he did. More so, he couldn't understand why Ginny, of all women, affected him this way.

Monte slapped him on the back. "Won't be long now; we'll be in business."

A trickle of excitement moved down Hayden's spine. They were going to catch mustangs! He'd dreamed of doing this for quite a while. Now it was becoming a reality. "I can't wait to start. Things will start snowballing before we know it," Hayden said.

Mustang Joe and Sam, followed by another ATV, pulled in beside them with the gas. The big man got down from the truck and moved to Hayden's side. "Well boss, we've got everything packed. Someone will need to sleep in the truck. That's too much gas to have around here with no one watching it."

Hayden nodded his head. "Take care of that."

Ginny huffed. "Are we going to jaw all day or get some work done?"

A chorus of 'yes ma'ams' followed her question.

Just as Hayden ducked his head to hide his laughter, a shot rang out and hit the truck beside him. Hell, there'd be an explosion if they hit the gasoline. He turned to see Mustang in the truck just ahead of him. Tires squealed and dirt flew as the truck took off, out of the way. Ginny stood still as if frozen. He rushed to her, grabbed her, and threw her over his shoulder. He was none too gentle as her body bounced against his own.

"Put me down. I'm perfectly capable of walking."

"You're supposed to run from gunfire." He made it to the barn and set her down. "Stay here," he commanded. He was surprised she had no comeback for his order. Opening the barn door a crack, he saw Cooper and Adam make a run for their SUV.

Monte joined him at the door. "They've got some drones. Those might help us find the perp faster than chasing after him."

"Chasing, hell. We still don't know where he's hiding." Hayden said. Whoever had fired the shot was nowhere to be seen. He ran flat out to the SUV and squeezed in beside Cooper. "Aren't you guys sitting ducks with all this glass? I want you wearing Kevlar."

"Read you loud and clear, buddy. The glass is bullet proof. We don't mess around with securing ourselves as well as our clients," Cooper said.

Adam tightened the wires on the drone, then turned to the laptop. It would control and direct the drones.

Cooper made the final adjustments to his own drone. "We've been lax so far. Sorry. We'll lock it down, starting now." He lifted the orb-shaped drone with feet and propellers.

Hayden admired the technology they'd often used on SEAL missions. While those had been a lot more sophisticated, these looked to be top of the line.

The two men stepped from the SUV, placed the drones on the ground, and finished adjusting the equipment. Hayden let his gaze roam over the landscape. "From the sound of the shot, it came from hills to the left of and behind the barn. Ginny, why don't you work with Cooper and Adam. You know all parts of the ranch and you can help them find the best hiding places."

She moved to the group cluttered around the electronics. He heard her ask, "Are you using sight only or measurements to navigate?"

Adam grabbed his chest in a comical pose. "Be still my heart. She speaks geek."

Cooper took her question seriously. "Since we don't have any aerial footage of the ranch or latitude and longitude measurements, this first time we will rely on visual. When you identify a landmark, we'll mark it. The computer will save all visual and map coordinates we find today."

He put on a head set and spoke into the mouthpiece. The drone lifted into the afternoon air with a lightness that belied its weight. Cooper leaned toward Ginny, pointing out things on the tiny screen. He guided the craft over the barns moving up and down testing the maneuverability of the drone.

Ginny pointed to the right of the screen. "Northeast of the second barn there are a couple of rocky outcrops with a few caves. From the top of one of the hills you could see the entire ranch very clearly."

Cooper handed the computer to Hayden. "I'm sure you'd like a look at your property."

Hayden took the pad and watched as Cooper moved the drone over the scattered pines and shrubs and to the outcrops. Green sprigs of grass and vibrant trees told of the richness of the property. "Hold it. Move left. I thought I saw something."

Cooper made the adjustment, and a cave came into view.

Hayden felt the adrenalin kick in. It felt good to be able to do something positive. "How close can we get?"

Since his arrival, he'd felt like he'd been chasing his tail. The image zoomed in on a spot of color on the ground. A soda can. Not the most incriminating evidence. Anyone could have ridden up the old trail and stopped at the cave. They'd have to check it out in person.

"I could find out much more if I see it, " Mustang said.

"Perfect. We don't want to let on we know where he's been hiding. Just the two of us, Mustang." Hayden checked his pistol and made sure he had an extra cartridge in his pocket. "The rest of you, take care of chores and pack your personal stuff for the trip tomorrow."

Jumping in the truck, he and Mustang took off."

Chapter Thirteen

It was mid-afternoon before the entire group completed preparations. Sam and another roust-a-bout left first to go ahead and set up camp. Hayden mounted Trigger, who was prancing in anticipation. Peyton and Monte rode work horses while Mustang and Ginny rode their own mounts. The air burned with the heat of the afternoon as leather creaked, horses danced, and people chatted.

Hayden pulled up alongside Ginny. "How long should it take to get there?" He tried to contain the eagerness in his voice but failed. This was an experience of a lifetime not to mention the launch of his new business.

She gave him a look of exasperation. "We just started so the answer is the same as the last time you asked. You're kind of cute all excited like this."

Hayden's breath caught. The words were fine, but the smile she sent him set him on fire. He was in deep trouble. She could turn him to putty with just a smile. Still, there was the pulled-up sheet to worry about and he wondered if she would ever trust him with her past. He returned her smile and dropped back to ride behind her.

An extra something seemed to hang in the air as Mustang took the lead and everyone fell into place behind him. Hayden wondered how many times this same scene had been played out through history. Of course, there'd been no ATV's back then, but today's outing was close enough to the past to bring a thrill. Fifty to a hundred years ago, this would have been a ritual carried out every spring. As cowboys they would not only catch the mustangs, but they also would have broken and trained them. Hayden tensed as Monte sped up to ride beside Ginny.

"Are you my boss, too?" Though the two rode in front of him, the challenge in her question brought Hayden's head up with a jerk.

"No. I'm not," Monte answered.

"You own half the ranch, don't you?"

Monte ran a hand around the neck of his shirt like it chaffed. "Not exactly. I own fifty percent of the horse breeding business. Hayden owns the ranch."

"That still leaves me as your employee, so you're my boss."

Monte threw a look over his shoulder that begged Hayden for help. With a shrug of his shoulders, he sped up and surged forward. Hayden eased in beside Ginny.

She wore a quirky look that said more about her attitude than her words. "Coming to his rescue?"

"Monte's a tough guy. He can stand on his own. I merely came up to find out more about what to expect."

"Dust. Lots of it. Mustangs will run for miles, feeding us dust the entire way. Other than that, you have the heat and bugs. The nicest part is the end of the day. As long as there's no snakes, I like sleeping on the ground."

"So, do you think I'll be able to catch a mustang on my first trip?"

"Don't feel bad if you don't. They're wily creatures and can twist out of the way in a heartbeat."

"Have you ever caught one?

"Almost. The rope landed crooked on his head, and he was able to twist out of it. It was a beautiful paint." She reached for her canteen and drank deeply. "I haven't been on another hunt since."

Hayden drank from his canteen also. "You love all this, don't you? Not just the training but all of it."

"Haven't you heard? The best way not to work is to do something you like."

"Don't make light of it, Ginny. Your face radiates your love every time you look at a horse. I admire that. Hopefully, one day I'll be just as happy."

Mustang held up his hand, signaling the horses needed a break. Everyone dismounted in the scarce shade of a scraggly pine. "Take fifteen and then we'll move on."

After dismounting, the old man pulled his lariat from his saddle. "I'll demonstrate some roping techniques while we're here. You're not exactly throwing the rope. You're swinging the loop until it starts to feel like it's pulling away from you in front. Release the loop and follow through across your chest to tighten the loop around the horses neck."

He demonstrated on a broken pine snag. Each time he released the loop, it glided smoothly across the space and landed around the target.

Hayden felt a twinge of worry. He was a fast learner and could complete nearly any task with practice. Hopefully this fifteen-minutes wouldn't be the only practice before they chased the mustangs. His heart thumped louder when Mustang handed him the rope for his turn to try. Conscious of all eyes upon him as he coiled the rope properly, he didn't like the idea of failing, especially in front of Ginny. He quieted his mind, breathed in and out a few times, then twirled the rope and let it go.

"Good job," Mustang said as the rope dropped into place on the pine. "Don't forget to follow through so you tighten the loop. You don't want your critter getting loose."

He let Monte and Peyton have a go, then signaled everyone to mount up. The trek continued.

****

Ginny held her breath as Hayden coiled his rope and began to swing. She wanted him to make it first time. Not that it mattered so much to her, but she knew how important it was to Hayden. He was so intent on making a success of this venture that she could feel his determination. When he threw and the loop landed on the pine, her muscles relaxed. She let out the breath she didn't realize she'd been holding. She might have known with his physical condition and reflexes, he'd do fine. Repeating the move while riding on a moving horse was the big question mark. She didn't have long to think about it as everyone mounted up and their journey continued.

She found herself riding beside Mustang and couldn't stop the questions burning in her brain. "What if we don't catch any?" She didn't realize she'd spoken the words aloud until Mustang replied.

"Have a little faith at least in me. We'll get some. How many is the question."

"But his plan depends upon it. We can't exactly create a new breed without horses."

My roustabouts can be counted on. I feel certain I'll catch at least one and Monte is experienced. You're worried *he* won't catch one, aren't you?"

Ginny looked away. Not only was Mustang the best tracker, but he also saw far too much in peoples' faces. "I admit, I want him to get his mustang. He deserves the chance to see his dreams come true."

"And what about your dreams? This ranch has been your salvation. You must feel resentment about being shoved aside."

"I did, at first. But now that I can see his vision, I want to be a part of it."

Mustang shook his head. "You're holding back both your resentment about the ranch and your feelings for the new owner."

Ginny gave her uncle a thoughtful look. He was a wise man. She did feel resentment—not just at Hayden, but at Austin. Why couldn't he have trusted her enough to confide his dreams to her? Had blood been the only thing that made him separate himself from her? She'd worked tirelessly for her dream. She wanted with all her heart for Wilcoyt Ranch to be successful. She didn't care how long the hours were or even how lonely the years had been. As long as she could work with the horses and live in freedom on the ranch, life was good.

Hayden had a mind of his own and wasn't including her in any of the decisions. How could she reconcile the anger and resentment with these new feelings she had for him?

Damn. When had that happened? Without realizing, she stopped her horse. How could she love him? He had no place for her in his plans.

"Ginny." Hayden's hand touched her arm.

She jerked as if drawn up by a string. Concern covered his face. Swallowing, she croaked, "What?"

"You're holding up traffic. I'd give you a penny for those thoughts, but I bet they're the five-dollar kind."

"Is that supposed to be funny?" she said gruffly. Desperately, she looked everywhere but directly at him. The knowledge of her love was too new. She didn't trust herself to keep him from seeing it in her eyes. She dug her heels into her horse's side and shot forward, catching up to the group. She'd have to watch herself around Hayden.

An hour later they turned a curve and climbed a little rise. Down below was a hollow, complete with pond and their camp completely set up. The smell of burgers and beans made her stomach growl. She heard the men all say something about starving. She rode to where the horses would be settled and began unsaddling her horse. The rest of the group copied her actions and a tired silence settled over them.

After brushing her horse down, she fed him some oats, then moved to the creek to rinse her hands and face. The cold water did much to revive her spirits as she watched the sun begin its descent into the distant hills.

Sam placed several plastic milk crates around the blazing fire and called, "Food."

Each time she tried to get into line someone pushed her into the lead. Finally, she acquiesced and grabbed a paper plate and accepted a burger from one of the roust-a-bouts. Placing a spoonful of delicious-smelling beans beside the burger she marched to the other side and picked her condiments. A few minutes later everyone was eating and enjoying the sunset.

Hayden pulled up a crate and sat beside her. "That had to be one of the best sunsets I've ever enjoyed."

Ginny looked at him in the flickering light. His eyes

shone with excitement. She could only imagine how he felt. The only times she'd felt that excited was at the birth of a foal or the arrival of a new mare at the ranch. This past year, after Austin's death, she'd been too busy trying to keep up with everything that needed to be done to feel much of anything. Her emotions had stayed frozen—until the night she and Hayden made love. Her pulse quickened at the memory. As a slight breeze brought his male scent to her, she felt her nipples harden in response. Quickly, she got up and threw her plate into the garbage bag.

Chapter Fourteen

Hayden watched as Ginny left so abruptly. Something had to be wrong, but for the life of him he couldn't figure out what. The trip had been uneventful, and he'd even proved himself somewhat adept at lassoing pines. Was she upset by her conversation with Monte?

"You're going to burn a hole into the side of that tent if you're not careful." Monte took the seat Ginny had vacated. "What's got you all in a stew?"

Hayden wiped a hand across his chin. "I'm not stewing. I'm closer to a boil."

Monte made a point of taking a closer look. "Oh-oh. I sense a storm brewing. What did she do to bring this on?"

"That's just it. She doesn't have to *do* anything. Just being around her ruffles my fur. My God, it nearly killed me to watch her bottom swaying on her saddle. This is the wrong time for crap like that, Monte. I can't get involved right now; the business has to come first."

"Aren't you being a little harsh?"

"On whom? Austin was the one who left me this predicament."

Monte threw a stick in the fire. "Now you're being pathetic. The Hayden I know would never admit defeat or run from trouble. What's gotten into you?"

A rustle in the brush momentarily caught Hayden's attention. When no other sound disturbed the quiet, he looked at his friend long and hard. "I'm not admitting defeat or fear of trouble. I'm just venting."

Monte threw back his head and laughed. "You've been bit. We'll see if it's fatal."

"Real funny," Hayden snarled. "Let's clear the table and play a few hands of poker."

Monte stood. "Nice change of subject but I'm willing to take your money."

"Did I hear cards mentioned?" Peyton moved from the other side of the fire. "I'll get Mustang. He can tell us some more unbelievable tales while we exchange funds."

****

Ginny stepped from the tent and made a nature call away from the sight and sound of the men. She'd left the fire because of how close Hayden had been sitting to her. His body heat alone made her ultra-aware of her feelings. She'd insisted on just-fun-with-no-strings-attached. Now she wished she had a few of those strings to hold on to. She'd get over this infatuation with him by the time he got his business up and running. She'd be damned if she'd let him make her uncomfortable enough to leave. Austin had said she had lifetime use of the ranch and she meant to stay.

My business comes first.

Hayden's words drifted through the night air. She sucked in a silent breath and moved farther away from the firelight and deeper into the shrubs. Without thinking, she moved to the creek, walking along the shadowed water's edge. This wasn't her first trip to this campsite, so she followed the creek West for fifteen or so minutes. The moon came out, lighting her way to her favorite spot. In the moonlight the small stack of falls glistened with sparkling water.

My business comes first.

Again, Hayden's words played in her head. She didn't doubt he'd spoken the truth. Her chest tightened and her eyes burned. Angry that she should be so upset, she stripped her clothes and waded in the creek waist high. The water was cold yet refreshing. She leaned back in the water, allowing her hair to splay out behind her. A Whip-Poor-Will called, sending a chill down her spine. The sound was so sad. Definitely not her favorite night bird. She settled her nerves by swimming around the falls.

Something rustled in the brush, sending her heart into overdrive. She wasn't normally afraid of night sounds, but she hadn't been paying attention to her surroundings. It could be a coyote or badger. Neither of which she'd like to tangle with tonight. She stopped swimming and watched the edge of the bank with eagle eyes. She saw movement, then a pair of boots. Her terror level subsided. She knew all the men out here and trusted them all.

"Ginny," Hayden called.

Now she was nervous. She was stark naked, and he stood between her and her clothes. She shouldn't be shy—they'd already made love, but something made her want to be clothed when she spoke to him.

"I'm here. What do you want?" Her words came out gruff and as unwelcoming as she could make them.

"What the hell, are you doing? There could be moccasins swimming in there. In the dark you couldn't see them."

Ginny sighed. Hayden definitely hadn't grown up in the country. People swam in rivers and creeks all the time. He was right about one thing, it w*as* dark. She had to give him some believable excuse or admit that she'd been stupid. "I'm in churning water. Snakes don't like it." She'd just made that up, but it sounded reasonable. She wasn't about to come running out of the water without clothes.

Hayden moved to the very edge of the creek. "How do you know what snakes like or don't like? Is that Native American knowledge or were you a girl scout?"

"Not funny, cowboy. Go back to your card game and let me get out."

He kicked off his boots, then pulled his shirt over his head. "I have a better idea."

Ginny closed her eyes. She'd seen him naked, but this seemed different.

His jeans hit the bank and he waded towards her. "I think you need protection."

She opened her eyes to find him mere feet from her. She wouldn't run. She didn't play games of chase. Her heart thumped faster. He wore a big smile. "I came to give you warmth."

She felt her own lips twitch. "I just bet you did. Who said I was cold?"

I saw your nipples when you leaned back in the water. They were very informative."

Ginny suppressed her grin as he gently bumped against her in the water. His hardness was no surprise, but it was definitely not reacting to the cold. His skin felt warm against her own. "Why so warm, Hayden?"

He bent closer and whispered in her ear. "You've got it wrong. I'm hot."

Once more his legs tangled with hers. She felt much warmer.

"Shall I share my heat?" he whispered.

Ginny went to push him away, but her hands ignored her commands and slid around his neck. Her fingers dug into the back of his hair. His breath feathered her skin, sending a shiver of pleasure down her torso and to her core. His mouth was so close she could clearly see his straight white teeth. Without thought, she pushed up and nipped him on those masculine lips. She had only time to see those firm lips turn into a grin before they covered hers in a playful kiss. She stilled; all playfulness gone as he deepened the kiss. When his tongue met hers, her body strained toward his. Her senses swam in a sea of sensation, pulling all sane thoughts from her mind.

Hayden pulled back and gave her a questioning look.

She didn't hesitate. Wrapping her arms around his neck she lifted her body, straddling his. His arms tightened around her back, slipping down to cup her bottom. As her body met his manhood a shiver of delicious tremors skittered down her spine. This was what she wanted. It didn't matter that he only cared for his business. She cared enough for the both of them. She stopped thinking when their bodies joined, and Hayden rocked her against him. This was a gentle joining. The movement of the water added another sensation. His lips now demanded as his tongue danced with hers. His gentle rhythm built a storm inside her core and fireworks exploded behind her eyelids. She felt his release and shuddered once more.

He said nothing and began walking to the edge of the creek. She tried to slide back down but his hands held her tightly against him. Before reaching the edge, he eased her to her feet and took her hand. Together they walked to the bank and silently donned their clothes.

"I'll leave first."

Hayden's words shattered her blissful peace. Her mouth tightened as anger flashed through her body. "Fine. Mustang will know where I've been, but no one else should."

Hayden pulled on his boots and straightened. "Will it bother you if the others know?"

Ginny shook her head. Before she could say anything, he bent and dropped a branding kiss on her lips. "I'll see you in the morning," He said and walked away.

Ginny was confused. She knew he wanted her, and she wanted him. Was that all there was to it? Not on her part, but he was unreadable. She shook her head to clear it and walked back to the camp.

Chapter Fifteen

The sun had barely peeked through the morning mist as Hayden awoke. Jumping up he made his way to the fire. Drawn to the smell of coffee, he poured a cup and grabbed a crate to sit on. Monte and Peyton were already awake and sat smirking at him.

"Did it rain last night?" Peyton asked.

Monte gave him a nudge with his elbow. "Must have. Hayden went to bed wet."

Hayden tried to hide his grin but couldn't. "Can't blame a man for wanting to stay clean."

Mustang Joe interrupted the banter. "A wild mustang waits for no one. Best hop to it."

The three men hopped up and grabbed a breakfast taco off the tray Sam had set out.

Hayden scarfed his down and made for his mount. His attention was caught when Ginny came up beside him already mounted. Her hair was pulled back in a ponytail and she was wearing sunshades. The hard line of her jaw, and tightly drawn up mouth, killed the good morning he'd nearly given to her. He swallowed any other comments and fell in beside Mustang Joe.

"Check your water." Mustang tapped his canteen. "We'll be out all day, and no one is drinking from the creek. We don't want anyone getting sick from tiny critters in the water. Check your ropes and double check your knots." He eyed each one in the group. " We'll only get one chance today. When I hold up my hand, everyone should ride full out and form a semi-circle. Whatever you do, don't rope the stallion. I don't want him to hurt himself trying to get away."

Peyton asked, "What do you do when you catch one?"

"Good question. Hand your catch over to Sam who will take them back to camp. Once you hand off, get right back into the chase." He laughed at their serious faces. "I'll buy a steak for anyone who catches one."

With his challenge given, Mustang turned his horse and cantered off. No one knew how long it would take to find the Mustangs so this could be a lengthy excursion.

Hayden tipped his head down and followed the tracker. Joe led them through territory covered with minimum vegetation. The calm, balmy air was eerily quiet--the only sound--the clops of horses' hooves. His breathing relaxed a little and he caught himself reliving last night. Ginny had been so beautiful in the moonlight. Her satiny skin glowed as he slid his fingers down the length of her arm. He forgot the talk of snakes and imagined dangers as her legs wrapped around his, slowly sliding upward. Something hit the back of his head. He turned and saw the grin on Peyton's face. He wanted to move back and bop his friend on the head in retaliation. Unfortunately, Joe held up his hand, then motioned for everyone to get down on the ground.

Joe belly-crawled toward the edge of the hill they'd just climbed. After looking over the edge, he motioned for everyone to come forward. Hayden was used to belly-crawling and quickly moved next to Joe. He sucked in a silent breath at the beauty that lay before him. Roans, Pintos, reds, blacks, and brown horses filled the space below them. There was a slight breeze and their manes and tails fluttered in the sunlight.

An Appaloosa moved from the center and came into his focus. He felt his heart lurch. That was the one. Not for the breeding program. He wanted that one for his own. He could hear the grass tearing as the animals grazed on the plush carpet of plants. No one moved or even whispered for fear of spooking them. The wind was in their favor just as Joe had hoped. He had to have scouted the area often to have known about this little copse of trees.

Joe motioned to the two roustabouts, and they moved off to the left and right of their location. He waited calmly and showed no signs of worry. He could have been a statue lying face down. Hayden, on the other hand, felt jumpy. His skin prickled and the hair rose on his arms. It was like how he felt before an op, tense and focused.

Joe sat up giving the sign to mount up. Everyone followed his lead.

Hayden's heart began to pound. He tried to hold back his excitement. Nothing had ever affected him this way. Except, Ginny. Making love to her was more than exciting; it was exhilarating. He pulled himself up and gave himself a mental jerk, and paid attention to Joe's signals. He moved up beside the scout as he dropped his hand.

Then everything happened at once. The horses sped forward in a jangle of tack. The mustangs sped down the hill in a blur of color and pounding hooves. The stallion, muscled and fierce, gave a wild cry to his harem. His mares turned as one and ran after him. Catching up to the running herd, Hayden looked for the Appaloosa. The spotted horse ran safely surrounded by the other mares.

Joe ran close to a beautiful red and threw his rope. With a hard jerk, the animal was pulled back toward him. Hayden swallowed his smile. He couldn't be distracted by admiration of Joe's prowess, or he'd lose his chance. Moving forward he encroached upon the group of mares. They parted, allowing him access to the center. There! The beautiful spotted horse was in front of him. He picked up his rope and kneed the sides of his mount.

The horse sped forward and he threw his lasso. The rope flew through the air and landed on the ear of the horse. Damn! He'd missed. The sound of hooves pounding around him was deafening. He choked on the dust as he frantically reset his rope. He'd dropped behind and the horse he wanted was up front, near the stallion. He pushed his horse, gathering speed. As he came alongside the Appaloosa, the stallion screamed and pawed the air with hooves coming dangerously close to his head. He reined his horse, preventing himself from running into the stallion. The herd flew around him. Clouds of dust blinded him as he looked for his quarry. Quickly, he kneed his mount as he bent over the horse's neck.

Coming up on the other side of the mare, he swiftly threw his lasso and said a quick prayer. He watched the rope stretch outward, hang in mid-air for a fraction of a second before plopping down over the horse's head. He pulled the rope taut and reined in his mount. The mare bucked and kicked as it screamed and fought. He felt a twinge of guilt. She would never run free again. Her cries pulled at something primitive in him and he felt a kinship with the animal. He swallowed hard and turned to find Sam. Reluctantly he handed the rope to the other man.

And just like that it was over. The men rode back toward him, four roped horses between them. Joe had managed to catch two of the four. Ginny drew up the rear, a smile as big as Texas on her face. "I got the black one. Isn't she beautiful?"

Hayden smiled back and clasped her on the shoulder in congratulations. He wanted to do more than that. He wanted to take her in his arms and kiss her senseless. She was like wine in his veins—intoxicating.

"Did you get one? "Ginny asked.

"Sure did. The prettiest Appaloosa you've ever seen."

Her face lit up. "I love Appaloosas. I can't wait to see her."

Hayden's phone rang. The music jarring in their natural surroundings. "Wilcoyt." He listened as Adam's voice explained they had another bullet fired at the ranch today. "Anyone hurt? How about the horses?"

He eased back in his saddle at the news everyone was okay, including the horses. "How are the new workers doing? I know they aren't trained but we need the help and they offered." Good. Check in at ten." He eased his phone back into his pocket. He faced the group who had stopped to listen to his conversation. "More shots were fired today. No one was hurt and the horses are fine."

Monte cursed; a few of the others chimed in with their thoughts.

Hayden kept his worry to himself as he prodded his horse forward. There'd be plenty of time for discussion when they got home. He jerked at the thought. When had he come to think of the ranch as home? He'd never called any place home except as a child. That place was gone now along with any ties he had to family. Wasn't that what *made* a home?

Arriving back at camp they were all drawn to the portable corral where the mustangs paced restlessly. Ginny drew up along the fence whispering to each of the animals. Hayden couldn't make out her words, but the animals seemed to calm in her presence. When she went to put a leg up on the fence, Hayden blocked her with his horse.

"What's the matter with you?" she snapped. "I'm trying to calm them."

"I'm just calming myself. You're not getting up on that fence."

The other men moved away from the scene, recognizing a storm brewing.

Ginny gave an exaggerated sigh. "I've been around wild horses before. This is my job."

"Not if you want to continue working for me. There are going to be some safety rules." Hayden hated the way he sounded. He knew it would put her back up, but he'd nearly had a stroke, imagining her beneath the hooves of those beautiful creatures.

"Hayden. You're being unreasonable."

"I'm being responsible. Can I trust you to take my 'no' as final instead of a challenge?"

Reluctantly she acquiesced. "Your Appaloosa is magnificent. What will you call her?"

"She's big for a mare. I'm going to keep her for my personal use." Hayden moved away from the fence and Ginny followed him." I'm not sure yet. Something that beautiful deserves a good name. I'll have to think on it."

He dismounted and unsaddled his horse. Sam took the animal and Hayden sat on a milk crate. The fire still blazed, though not as fiercely as it would tonight. Tonight, there would be stories swapped, a few beers consumed, and talk of tomorrow's chase. A buzzing noise interrupted their quiet. Spooked, the horses began jumping and kicking. Hayden looked up and saw something flying in the distance. "What the hell is Cooper up to? He should know better than to fly that thing over us."

"That's not one of ours," Peyton said. "Someone else is surveying us."

"Shoot it down before the mustangs break out." His words barely left his lips and Joe angled his rifle up and shot the machine. Electric sparks flew everywhere as the machine began to spin out of control. Everyone ducked as the drone made a mad arc above them before slamming into a boulder.

"Everyone, okay?" Hayden asked as his friends uncurled themselves from their hunched positions. All but Ginny answered in the affirmative. Noticing her lack of response, Hayden rushed over and saw her cradling her arm.

"A piece of the burning drone broke off and hit me."

Moving her hand out of the way, Hayden looked at the nasty burn on her arm. Peyton reached over his shoulder, handing him the first-aid kit. The wound was confined to a two-inch mark on her forearm. "These look like first and second-degree burns. You should be fine."

Hayden tore open a medical wipe and cleaned the burn as gently as he could. Ginny jerked her arm and sucked in a pained breath. He paused in his ministrations. "Pack up everyone, we're going back." He looked to Joe to confirm his words.

Joe called to his men and the camp began to look

like a nest of ants. He turned back to Hayden. "We'll need to take it slow. Our horses and the mustangs ran hard today."

"I understand. I just don't like strangers spying on me. I'm also worried about the ranch. If these people have drones, they can know the location of any of our people. No, we've got to get back there."

"It's normally a three-hour ride from here to the ranch. Without cutting our speed will have us arriving after dark."

Hayden saw the worry in Mustang Joe's finely lined face. Driving horses in the dark was dangerous. His worry over the danger his people were in at the ranch kept him silent. Mustang might be worried, but he was the best horse person he knew, besides Ginny. They'd just have to be careful. He had a bad feeling about the ranch. They had to get back quickly. Tying the wrap loosely around Ginny's arm, he prevented himself from dropping a kiss on the bandage. Instead, he jumped up. "I'll take care of your things."

"But I can—"

He was gone.

Chapter Sixteen

Hayden sighed. They faced a long, hot, ride and little conversation. He dropped back to ride next to Ginny. She'd lost her earlier excitement and her shoulders slumped. Her attention was held by the five mustangs. They were skittish and she spent her time riding near one and then the other. Her voice was husky from gentling the wild horses. She took a long swig of water.

"How are things going?" Hayden asked?

Ginny put the top back on the canteen, "Okay. I'm a little worried about stress strokes. After the long runs, fear and capture, these animals should be resting."

Dry lightning flashed in the east and the animals whinnied and jerked at their ties. Everyone pitched in with soft words of comfort. Another bolt flashed in the sky. Hayden eyed the sky, worry consuming him. "Will the lightning be a problem?"

"Not necessarily. I'm more concerned about the gusty winds these storms generate. They can produce dust storms."

Hayden nodded and moved his horse up in the line beside Joe. "Ginny's worried about the winds associated with the dry lightning. How long before we reach the ranch?"

"I saw that last flash," Joe said. "We're about an hour from the ranch. It's hard to tell how fast the storm is moving. We could ride faster and err on the side of caution."

Hayden thought for a moment. "I think the risk is worth it. I'd hate to lose the animals in a dust storm."

Joe urged his gelding to a fast walk, and everyone picked up the pace. Lightning flashed again, this time much closer.

Hayden pulled out his cell and called Cooper. "Hey, we're almost home. There could be a dust storm coming. Put all the animals in the stables and button down the barn. Make sure there's hay in the new stalls." He listened a moment. "We'll be there in thirty minutes. He pushed the button to end the call, wondering if he'd remembered everything.

"Remember, there are three extras to stay over, if need be," Joe said calmly. People can double up. Each of the bunk house rooms has two beds in it."

"Thanks. I'm not sure I would have remembered housing situations. Let me know anything else I might be forgetting.

"You're doing fine, boss. Don't forget to ask for help when you need it. Ginny is a fountain of knowledge. She's forgotten more about ranching than most men know. Let her help." Joe shut up and started humming a song.

Hayden grinned. That was the end of Joe's lecture. Short and to the point. He *had* been pushing her to the background. Damn Austin. He should have left the ranch to her. At least he could have made them equal partners. None of this mattered if they didn't get this mess solved so the thoroughbred could arrive. The paddocks came into view. His grip on the reins eased and his back relaxed. He couldn't control every situation but being in the midst of the action made him calmer.

Cooper and Adam met them outside the barn. Both men took one of the mustangs. Ryan grabbed the reigns of Ginny's horse and she dismounted. She tightened the rope on the black mustang and pulled it toward the barn. The mare screamed and reared on her hind legs. Immediately Joe moved to help her.

An eerie feeling charged the air. Hayden had been through too many hurricanes in Florida to not recognize that sense of waiting. The storm was close. Too close. He dismounted and went into the barn. He smelled the fear in the air. The animals were frightened of the impending storm and the mustangs. The smell of new wood and hay greeted him as he entered the new addition. Everyone was busy working with a horse.

Hayden checked the Appaloosa's water, grabbing the hose to add more. Adrenalin dried the horses out and they would drink deeply. "You probably have time to make it home, Mustang. If you can spare them, your men can stay and help."

"No, I'm needed here. Someone must stay in the barn with the animals. What do you want to do with the work horses? That barn isn't as secure as this one."

"I told Ryan to bring them over here. Let's put them as far from the mustangs as you can. Hayden turned to Adam who was talking softly to the brown mustang. "Don't get too close. She'll take a bite out of you."

Adam laughed. "She's female, right?"

"Females bite, remember?" Hayden reminded him of his last foray with a female.

Ryan came through the back door with two of the work horses. "Hey boss. Sam and I got the last four out."

"Good work. Get them settled with the rest.

Chapter Seventeen

The storm arrived fast and furious. Everyone stayed in the main barn. Noel fixed a big pot of chili and brought it over before moving to the bunkhouse with her family. Dust seeped through cracks as the wind howled, blowing sand and debris at the buildings. The older barn rattled with each gust; the horses whinnied at the noise. The new stud barn held up better. The extra supports designed to take a stallion's angry hooves, now served them well against the storm.

Hayden put his empty bowl in the basket the housekeeper had left for that purpose and walked into the older barn annex. Horses nickered nervously, stamping their hooves. He stopped at the first stall and ran a hand down Rebecca's face. She nuzzled him back, then jerked back when an especially strong gust of wind slammed into the building. He calmed her with soothing words before moving onto the other stalls.

Edgy, he moved away from the horses to sit on a bale of hay. His mind darted, finally fixing on the root of his fear. If the storm was bad enough, he could lose everything. Monetarily, it didn't bother him. He was young and could start over—but his dream. And what about Ginny? She could find work on any ranch with her horse skills but would hate it. Wilcoyt Ranch was her life. He had to keep it going.

Joe came up beside him. "These things can be bad

but don't usually last long." In the distance, a sudden roar sounded, changing the older man's tone. "Everyone, get down!" he bellowed. "That's a twister."

Hayden ducked behind the bale of hay and waited. The barn shuddered. He held his breath as dust billowed in from cracks between the boards. Tension in the barn mounted. With an ungodly shriek, a sheet of tin ripped from the roof. A loud snort came from Jasmine's stall, and she kicked the gate to her stall.

Monte and Sam grabbed her halter and tried to calm her. She continued to kick.

"Throw a blanket over her back," Ginny yelled.

Hayden jumped up to grab a blanket from the rail. Throwing it across the horse's back, he stood back, out of the way of her hooves. Jasmine calmed and the kicking stopped.

The horrendous sound moved past but was followed by an explosion just north of the barn. Hayden moved quickly to calm one, then another of the horses. He thought furiously. What had it destroyed? Then it hit him: the workhorse barn. God, he was glad they'd moved the horses.

Once the wind died, everyone rushed outside. Boards from the bunkhouse lay strewn across the yard along with the tin from the barn. The house was intact, but it had weathered many such storms in the past. Everyone's eyes focused on the workhorse barn. What had been an old but sound structure, now lay in haphazard clumps of wood and tin. The entire structure had collapsed.

Hayden counted himself lucky. The barn had needed replacing anyway. They would have to work fast to get another one built in the next few days. He wanted nothing to stand in the way of the stallion coming.

Ginny walked over to stand beside him. "We could let the horses out a few at a time to release some of their stress. Between the arena and the paddocks, we could accommodate the mares and work horses. The mustangs had best stay where they are."

Hayden nodded. "All right. Let's get started."

By the time the sun crested the hills in the east the horses had been settled. Hayden dragged a weary arm across his brow and walked toward the house. The smell of breakfast cooking reminded him that Noel was still here. He hoped that she and her family had gotten more sleep than the rest of them.

"Breakfast in twenty minutes," she chimed.

Hayden poured himself a mug of coffee, swallowing half of it before replying. "Sounds good. I'll be in the office."

He walked to his room, ignoring the bed that called to him. There was no time for sleep now. He sat at the desk and picked up the phone. Flipping the pages of the phone book, he found what he was looking for and punched in the number. "Hello. Yes, this is Hayden from the Wilhoyt Ranch. I need a work crew over here immediately. I don't give a damn about schedules. My barn was destroyed last night, and it must be replaced in three days. Dammit, charge me extra if that's what it takes."

He slammed the phone down. He sensed someone behind him and turned to find Ginny leaning against the frame. "You catch more flies with honey," she said.

"I find you catch more with money. If that doesn't work, I'm not above a little coercion."

Ginny raised a brow. "I'm going to catch the shower

first. You need anything before I do?"

"By any chance are we insured for the barn?" Considering the ranch's finances, he doubted the insurance had been kept up.

"Austin was a fanatic about insurance. The papers are in the file cabinet. Look under Fosters. That's the name of the company. Anything else?"

Hayden turned back to the desk. "Go enjoy your shower. I've got things to keep me busy."

He knew she would rush through her shower and be back in the barns in thirty minutes. No way would she shirk her duties. Trying not to think of the steamy water pouring over her tanned skin he waited until he heard her footsteps in the hall, then groaned. His chest and abdomen were killing him. He should be resting but didn't have the time. He moved to his duffel bag and shook two ibuprofens from the bottle. His eyes landed on the bottle of pain killers. It was unopened. He studied the pills thoughtfully, then shoved them deeper into the depths of the bag. He'd born the pain since leaving the hospital. He could damn well do it now.

"Breakfast!" Noel called from the kitchen.

He ignored the call and rifled through the file cabinet until he found the Fosters file.

"Hayden?" Monte spoke from the doorway. "That file will still be there when breakfast is over. Come and eat."

"I was just checking our insurance. There's a possibility we could be covered for storm damage."

"Good. Now, let's eat."

Hayden hesitated. There was so much to do. At Monte's impatient look he followed him to the kitchen. Everyone was seated around the table or at the counter.

Noel placed heaping bowls of bacon, hash browns, scrambled eggs, and biscuits on the table. The housekeeper handed him a plate filled to overflowing. He ate two biscuits standing up before moving to the living room couch.

Monte joined him. "I'm thinking of asking for a leave of absence."

"What?" Shocked, Hayden turned to his friend. "What reason are you going to give this man's navy?"

Monte crunched a piece of bacon before answering. "I'm going to say I have a brother who needs my help."

"Dammit, Monte. You're an only child."

"But you're my brother."

The simple words nearly choked Hayden up." He cleared his throat. "I can do this without sacrificing your career."

"A leave of absence is not a career ender. After we get things cleared here and the business is up and running, I'll go back. I love working on the teams."

Hayden looked his friend in the eye, searching to see his sincerity. "I'll be happy to have you then."

"I'll fly back to the base tomorrow and then go pick up the stallion from there."

****

Later that afternoon a call came in from the lawyer.

"Hello, Hayden." Allister Branson's voice sounded in his ear.

"Allister, what can I do for you?"

"Well, son. It seems there is another wrinkle in our situation. After research I found some evidence of another possible claim to the property.

"Who?" Hayden didn't care if he sounded abrupt. If he had to fight tooth and nail for his ranch, he would.

"The word of mouth by which I received this news, says Ginny's grandmother was once married to Austin."

"Then Ginny gets the ranch?" He felt gut-punched. He didn't mind sharing his dream with her, but if she got the ranch, she might not want to share with him.

"That remains to be seen. Native American marriages to white men weren't always recognized as legal back then."

"What do I need to do?"

"Talk to her. She'd know about this. Maybe there's some paperwork that proves or disproves this. Sorry I don't have better news."

"That's okay. We'll deal with it." Irritation flooded his body, but he managed to say a polite goodbye before hanging up.

If Ginny knew about this all along, and had the paperwork to prove it, why not tell him right away? Money. She didn't have the capitol to develop the place.

As soon as the thought entered his mind, he shoved it aside. Ginny was as honest as they came. She had to have some other reason to hide the information from him. They needed to talk. Shaking his head, he failed to clear it. He needed to step back from everything and get a new perspective. He'd take Trigger for a ride.

Opening the box that contained Austin's stuff, he picked up the little scrap of paper and the handful of rocks. The paper contained circles and lines—maybe a map? Austin had a source of income not shown in his books. This little drawing could hold the key to finding it. The only recognizable part was the teardrop which had to be the little lake. Time for some sleuthing.

****

Feeling refreshed after her shower, Ginny entered

the kitchen. Finding Noel peeling potatoes, she grabbed another knife and joined her. There was something relaxing about chopping vegetables. Since they didn't kick or bite at you, it made for a nice change. Noel left her to it and went into the locker. Ginny thought of the giant cold storage and grimaced. She'd accidentally locked herself in one time. She always left the door open now, regardless of how much cold escaped.

The door opened and Joe came in.

Ginny looked up. "I thought you had gone."

Joe moved to the ever-hot pot of coffee. "I stopped in town on the way home. I heard a rumor and thought you might want to know."

"I certainly don't want to hear any gossip. People put too much stock in it"

"True, but this one concerns you. They're saying your grandmother was married to Austin. That would make a case for you to claim a part of the ranch"

"You should know more about it than I. Besides, if Austin had wanted me to own the ranch, he would have left it to me"

"Maybe you could visit your mother and find out."

Ginny froze. Her fist bunched, whitened knuckles stood out against her dark skin. Her heart began to pound. Dear God, this couldn't be happening. She'd buried everything for years. Why was it rearing its ugly head now?

Her voice, when it came from her tightened throat, was husky. "I have no interest in raking over dead ashes. I'm content with things the way they are."

Joe took a long swig of coffee. "You deserve this place, Ginny. You kept everything together and running smoothly. You were also Austin's only company. Surely you deserve some repayment."

"You don't get it, do you?" she bellowed. "I loved that old codger, despite his disrespect of my sex."

"The tribal council would stand behind you if you wanted to try."

Hands shaking, she placed the knife on the counter. "Where the hell was the tribal council when I was thirteen? Why didn't someone do something then?"

"I'm sorry. I didn't mean to dredge up old pains. I'll go help in the barn."

Joe drained the coffee cup and without a word, left the house.

With her mind in turmoil, Ginny picked up the knife and began cutting up the potatoes. She tried to send her spinning thoughts to the dark edges of her mind, but it didn't work. Tears pricked her eyes and she felt panic quicken her breaths. She dropped the knife and ran outside. Not giving herself time to think, she entered the barn and moved to the mares' stalls.

Within a few minutes, she had Brandy saddled. Mounting, she moved toward the end of the new barn where the men were working. "I'm heading out for a quick ride to clear my head. I'll be back in an hour."

Monte put down the bag of horse feed. "Shouldn't someone go with you? People are shooting at us remember?"

"I'll be fine. Where's Hayden?"

"He took Trigger for a ride," Ryan said. "He's been gone about a half hour."

"See, I won't be alone."

She turned the horse and exited the barn before anyone could stop her. Ginny settled into the saddle and slapped Brandy on the rump. The horse took off at a gallop. Wind ripped at her hair, cooling her face. She was mentally and physically exhausted. She needed a little break and the horse needed exercise. All the horses had been cooped up too long in the stables. Maybe she'd have time when she got back to exercise some of the others.

Twenty minutes later, she slowed the mare to a walk. Unconsciously, she'd headed for the lake. The cool blues and greens gave the place almost a tropical appearance. The reflections cast by the brush and few trees rippled in the sun. A little dip in the water would be a perfect end to an overly long day.

She tied Brandy to a sturdy branch on one of the trees. Her clothes were off in no time. Ginny dove into the water with a loud splash. Her body registered the coolness of the water, but her mind ignored it. This was heavenly. Closing her eyes, she floated on the lake's surface. Something bumped her and she startled. Before she could take a breath, she was pulled under.

She fought against the hands holding her and managed to break the surface, gasping to catch her breath. "Hayden! Are you trying to drown me?"

"I didn't mean to frighten you. I thought you saw me in the water."

"Well, I didn't."

She allowed him to hold her upright while he treaded water. That's when she noticed they were both naked. Her stomach tightened as a frisson of desire raced through her. His eyes studied her, and she knew the instant he became aware of her intimately. His pupils widened and the flecks of gold sparkled. Her breath hitched. His mouth descended toward hers. Anticipation heightened her arousal. Hands that pushed him away, now roamed over his muscular chest.

She moved both hands over his tight abs, pausing when she came to his scars, caressing the puckered skin with gentle fingers. "This nearly killed you. Didn't it?"

Hayden caught her hand and pulled it up for a kiss. "It did kill part of me. Working with the teams has been my life. I'll heal, but that part of my life is over."

"You've got a new life now, and I am happy you're here." She pulled her hand free and wrapped it around his neck. "Hayden?"

"Hmmm?" he murmured in a husky voice.

Her hand wrapped in his hair and pulled his head down. She feathered little kisses over his face and whispered, "You talk too much."

It was as if she'd said some magical word. His gaze pierced her own, showing her his intent. His mouth came down on hers in a hard, demanding kiss. She responded in kind, kissing him back ferociously. His mouth opened over hers, demanding her surrender. Their tongues met, sending lightning spears of need down her body. His arm slid beneath her as he moved them toward the bank. He laid her gently on the clothes she'd left on the shore. The world disappeared as their lovemaking became frenzied.

"I can't wait long," he rasped.

"Then don't."

His arms tightened, binding her to him as he entered her with one deep thrust. She came as soon as he breached her opening. Rather than savor the feelings her body began another assent. When she could stand it no longer, she shattered around him.

He plunged into her one last time and shuddered his release. Moments later Hayden held her tightly against him and rolled onto his back. She was on top looking down into eyes that beguiled her. Her fingers gently roamed his face. "We've got to get back. Someone will come looking for us."

Hayden heaved a sigh. "You're right."

Ginny understood his reluctance. She'd like to spend the entire afternoon making love and swimming in the lake. There were too many issues between them for that to happen. She waited for him to roll off her clothes, then quickly dressed. "Where's Trigger? That's why I didn't see you when I rode up."

"I left him in the shade down the bank a little."

She gathered her horses' reins and walked down the bank. Trigger stood munching grass and flowers from the bank. Ginny mounted her horse and the two rode toward home.

Chapter Eighteen

Hayden propped his foot on the fence and sipped coffee from his mug. He was glad he'd continued his early morning date with sunrise. To him it was the best part of the day--especially today. By this afternoon, his stallion would be here. He'd debated long and hard about going ahead with his plans until the shooter was caught. One well-placed bullet could ruin his plans for a stud farm and new breed. He'd weighed the pros and cons and decided to go ahead with their plans. Monte had agreed. They'd just have to be careful about keeping the horse out of sight. No problems, it should be easy to hide a horse on a horse ranch. He caught the sound of a whistle in the arena. Ryan must be getting a jump on the day's work. He poured the last dregs of his coffee out and made his way inside.

Adam was the first to greet him. "Morning, boss."

All the chairs were full as Hayden approached the table. Grabbing a plate, he filled it, and walked to the wall, leaning his tall frame against it. "Today's the big day, boys." He looked around the table and spotted Ryan. "I thought you were working in the arena. Who's out there?"

He didn't really need to ask. Ginny never missed a moment to work with the new horses. Without pausing for a breath, he bit out the next question. "Who's with her?" At the blank looks he dropped his plate on the counter and whirled toward the door. He stopped a foot away and turned to the group. In a steely voice he growled, "Ginny is not to work alone with the mustangs. Do I make myself clear?"

"Yes, boss," the men chorused.

Hayden flung the door open and headed for the barn. His anger hadn't cooled during the short walk. Tension coiled across his shoulders when he turned the corner to the arena. It wasn't anger that tightened his body. She was beautiful. Her black hair hung across her shoulder in a thick braid. Her skin glowed golden in the filtered light. The horse was just as beautiful. The Appaloosa's color was perfect.

His heart quickened at the memory of capturing the gorgeous creature. To see her next to Ginny was a picture only Remington could have captured on canvas. He stood transfixed until Ginny stopped working the animal. He waited until she handed the horse off to Ryan who appeared as if by magic at her side. Rather than stay in the arena, he walked out into the paddock.

She followed him, walking slowly.

"I gave strict orders that you were not to work with the mustangs alone."

"No one else understands them like I do."

"I agree. I also know you're the best horse whisperer around. That doesn't negate the order."

"But—"

"Dammit, it's for your safety. You know I don't budge on safety issues."

Ginny stared back at him defiantly but couldn't hold his gaze. She looked down and said, "I know. I'm still not used to taking orders instead of giving them."

"The men will be the ones who pay for your mistake

on this issue. They know better." He stared into her warm brown eyes and saw the flint of anger. "If you have a problem with my orders, come to me. I'll make them crystal clear."

He turned away before he said too much and went to the new barn where the stallion would be housed. Excitement burned his anger away and he went about checking everything for the hundredth time. Everything was ready to go. Soon he'd have the mustang mares mated and his new breed would be born. He also wanted to breed the six other mares and create an upscale riding horse at a lower price.

The rumble of wheels over rough road heralded the arrival of the stallion. All hands stopped, watching as the large truck and trailer pulled into the yard. A billow of dust had nearly settled when the driver's door opened. Monte stepped from the truck, pushing his Stetson back on his head.

Hayden's stomach tightened in anticipation as he walked to meet his friend. Grabbing Monte's hand, he squeezed and pulled the big man in for a hug.

Monte laughed and patted him on the back. "I didn't know you'd miss me this much."

"I missed the horse, not you." Hayden stepped back and headed for the trailer gate. A solid kick landed against the gate as he approached. "Looks like someone's ready to see their new home."

Hayden waited for Monte to hand him the key before unlocking the padlock and lowering the ramp. "Which end do you want?" Monte asked.

"I'll take the head. You get those powerful looking hind legs."

Monte shrugged and flashed Hayden a smile. A

small crowd had gathered but remained at a safe distance from the pounding hooves. The stallion became agitated and tried to buck in the small space. "Grab his chinstrap and yank his head down. Push back on his head with your chest. Be careful, you'll be between him and the wall of the trailer. Don't let him pen you."

"Now, you tell me," Hayden groused. He did as he was told and held the horse's head low. The horse seemed to accept his fate and settled down.

Monte jumped up behind the stallion and eased a rope on one of the hind legs. "Put your rope on his head and hold on."

Hayden pushed the horse back toward the end of the trailer. Elated when the horse responded appropriately, he continued to keep the horse's head down as he pushed it toward the gate. The horse stumbled as it reached the downward slope. Several others jumped in to push the animal to its feet. Within moments the large equine stood before the group, pounding his hooves on the ground. From the side, Peyton lassoed the horse and pulled the rope tight.

"Let's get him under cover," Monte yelled over the horse's shrieks.

Together the two men with ropes walked forward as the leg rope was removed.

Hayden grunted. The horse reminded him of a steam engine all heated and ready to go. Adrenaline pumped through his veins as he moved the muscle-packed animal forward. Reaching the barn, he led the horse to the reinforced section designated for the stallion. He led the animal into the large stall and then jumped onto the fence. There was too much space for him to stay in the stall. The powerful stallion could easily trample someone. Sam and Monte closed the gate as Hayden removed the rope from the horse's neck.

Finally, after the animal was secured, and Hayden's dream could begin to unfold. "Monte, check his hind legs. He wasn't limping from that stumble, but it's best to make sure."

Monte moved into the stall, carefully dodging a well-placed kick. When the horse settled, he ran a practiced hand down the animal's hind legs. "Looks good but we'll keep an eye on them."

Cooper filled the water bucket as Ginny slipped in and placed some oats in the feed bag. Hayden looked up. "Ginny, you are not to work with the stallion. You can give advice from the sidelines, but no direct contact."

Her eyes flashed hotly at him, and she turned away and left. He turned to look at each of the men beside the fence and said, "Your job is to see that order carried out." At the nods and yeahs, he was satisfied he'd made his point. "This calls for a celebration. Cooper, you take first watch while the rest of us have a beer. I'll send you one."

Cooper nodded and turned back to watch the stallion.

****

Hayden stepped out of the walk-in fridge, a couple of six packs in his hands. Passing the beer around, he grinned as congratulations were expressed and hands pounded his shoulder. He swore that his heart would burst if he got much happier.

He'd worked hard to overcome his medical status so this dream would be possible. Now, he only had to find whoever was terrorizing the ranch and get the business up and thriving. It would be several long years before it would start paying anything back. He and Monte had their work cut out for them to keep the place on solid ground.

As he handed Ginny a beer, her eyes met his. Tension sparked between them. The smile on her face said one thing and the cold look in her eyes said something else. It had been too long since they had talked. Hell, they'd never really talked. Somehow, they ignited when they touched leaving no time or thought for conversation. He had to reach her. Each time she slashed him with a look, the hurt in her eyes nearly killed him.

Hayden broke the silence between them. "It's really happening."

"Yeah," she said. "You deserve it."

Her words said she approved but did she mean it? Her eyes showed the gamut of emotions. "So do you. You've worked harder than three men the last few weeks. You should also celebrate for yourself."

"I have no reason to cheer other than I'm happy for you."

"Nonsense. You're as much a part of this as Monte or myself."

"I'm just an employee, remember?"

"Dammit, Ginny. You know you're a critical part of this operation."

"I don't want to argue when you should be celebrating. The men need to see you. It will affirm their hard work and the risks they've taken with their lives."

"Look, I know I have to mix with the men, but we need to talk. Promise me that we can talk before going to bed."

She stared back at him for several tense moments before smiling. "All right. We can talk but you also need to listen. You may have your stallion and all the preparations for the business, but this isn't over. Jason Lancaster doesn't give up easily."

Hayden took a pull on the bottle of beer. "I know, and I'm prepared for that."

She ran the bottle across her forehead. "I hope so." Turning away, she moved to join the others.

Hayden tapped his pocketknife against the beer bottle. Quiet descended upon the group. "I'd like to thank all of you for your hard work and sticking with me. I propose a toast. To Salvadore and the future of this venture."

Bottles tapped and everyone took a swig of their beers. Ginny took a sip of hers and then disappeared down the hall.

Hayden tried not to let her departure bother him. This was a celebration; yet it took all his willpower to keep from running after her. She had a right to be here—maybe more than he. She was so damn stubborn. Why couldn't she see how much he wanted her to be part of this. The beer lost its' flavor and he set it aside. All he could hope for was their promised talk tonight.

Chapter Nineteen

Ginny shucked off her work clothes, put on her robe, and headed for the bathroom. The hot water pounding against her flesh relaxed the tension in her shoulders. She was angry with herself. How could she have behaved so badly? Hayden deserved this celebration. He'd worked hard to build up the ranch. Granted she and the others had worked just as hard. The men were getting better pay and she didn't have to make all the tough decisions. There it was. The reason behind her inability to join Hayden in his excitement. She didn't get to make any of the decisions. To his credit, Hayden did ask for her opinion and deferred to her when it came to training the horses. She sighed and turned off the faucet. No amount of hot water could ease that throb. Somehow, she had to come to terms with the new chain of command.

In her room, she changed into clean jeans and a simple camp shirt. She left the shirt untucked, liking the loose fit. She was about to comb and braid her hair when a knock sounded at her door. She put down the comb and turned to face the door. "Who is it?"

"It's Hayden. May I come in?"

Her heart raced. Why was he here?

"Ginny?"

She moved to the door and opened it a crack. "What do you want? We agreed to talk tonight."

I've got some time before supper and thought it

might be better to talk now."

He wasn't wearing his Stetson and his hair lay flat against his head. It gave him an endearing look. Her fists clenched. She couldn't think such thoughts and keep her mind on the issues between them. "I'll meet you in the office." It was the most unromantic place she could think of. There was still a bed. She closed the door and shook her head. She had to focus, or she'd be grabbing him and kissing those perfect lips.

Minutes later she knocked on the office door.

Hayden turned from the desk. "Come in, Ginny." He stood and offered her the chair. He pulled out another chair borrowed from the kitchen and sat.

Impatient, she swiveled the chair and spoke. "What exactly do you want to talk about?"

Hayden cleared his throat. "Us." His voice was husky. "I don't think you're right when you call this thing between us just sex. The feelings I have for you go beyond sex."

Ginny's heart picked up its pace at his words. "Isn't sex what men want?" Her jaw tightened and her face took on a belligerent look.

Hayden chuckled. "Damn right. For most men. Some want more than just a romp in the hay. I happen to be one of them.

"Why? Things would be so easy if we left it alone."

"It has gone too far for that. We have something between us."

"You can't say that you love me. We've only known each other for a couple of months."

Hayden sighed. "Time doesn't matter, Ginny. Everyone experiences love differently. Do you have feelings for me?"

Panic raced through her body. She didn't want to tell him anything and didn't have to. She knew he'd end things if she didn't share. "I don't know what they are, but yes, I do feel something more."

Hayden gave her a smile and a nod. "Enough said. We'll let things play out. Now, I have another matter to discuss. Was Austin married to your grandmother?"

"What?" What was she supposed to tell him? Yes, and have him question the legality of his claim? She didn't even know if the proof still existed. She couldn't lie to him. There was no way they could have anything together based on lies.

Hayden ran a hand around his neck then swiped his forehead. "You heard me. It's all the rumor around town. Why wouldn't you tell me something this important?"

Ginny rubbed her sweaty palms across the fabric of her jeans. "First, I haven't heard the rumors. Second, I'm not sure there's proof they were married. Native marriages to white men weren't recognized back then."

Hayden jumped to his feet and paced the office. "So, it's true."

"There is a slight possibility. Like I said, I can't verify it. The proof if any exists, will be found on the reservation."

He jumped at her words. "Get your purse, we're going to the reservation."

"You can't just show up on the rez without calling ahead. The people we need to see might not be there." Panic once again seized her lungs and her breath caught. She wasn't ready to face her past.

"What's wrong? Why are you breathing funny?"

Coldness covered her skin as Hayden's words feathered her face. Her head began to spin as darkness edged into her vision. Moments later, strong hands pulled her shoulders forward and pushed her head between her knees. His harsh words tempered and became murmurs of concern. "It's all right. Just take it easy. You're going to be okay."

Ginny felt the air rush back to her lungs as the blood pushed back into her head. "I'm fine. You can let me go."

"Could have fooled me. You looked like death just now. I lost five good years of my life as your eyes rolled back into your head. Does this happen often?

"No. I don't know what came over me."

"Liar. You just happen to faint while we are talking about your past? You need to come clean this time, Ginny. No more hiding things. Your past will take away from your future—if you let it."

Her head jerked up, defiance in her face. "It's easy for you to say. You're not the one with secrets so dark they can barely be spoken. I can't go back there. I just can't." He took her hands, and she stifled the urge to jerk them back.

"Easy. I understand this is hard for you but you're letting it rule your life."

"It's my life, dammit. I was muddling along just fine before you showed up." He rubbed her hands and she grasped at the warmth of his flesh.

Hayden sighed. "I'll be right there with you. No one will harm you. Now, can you share your past with me. Remember those feelings we have between us. I need to understand why you're so against feeling close to someone."

Her chin lifted. "All right. You asked. When I was about ten, my father came to my bedroom and tried to kiss me." Her voice at first defiant, dropped to barely above a whisper. Her words became halting. "He—he said it was a secret and I wasn't to tell my mom. I… pushed him away. Then he …he hit me. I tried to scream but he covered my mouth with his hand. He said that if I said a word, he'd beat her." Her mouth became dry, and she swallowed hard.

Hayden's voice interrupted gently. "Did you tell your mother?"

Her gaze dropped to her lap. "Not at first. I believed him and didn't want my mom hurt. When he kept coming to my room, I told her."

"And?" Hayden asked softly.

"She didn't believe me. Or at least she said she didn't. Looking back through the eyes of an adult, she must have known."

"Go on."

"Off and on through the years he kept coming to my room. Sometimes he hit me and the others he tried to force his attentions. I didn't know what to do so I went to a council member. He laughed and said I had an active imagination.

Hayden snorted in disgust.

Her words halted and her breathing became more ragged. "One day when I was fourteen, my mom was out shopping. I didn't realize he was at home. I started taking my shower and the door burst open. I tried to cover myself with the shower curtain, but he ripped it from the rod. His eyes took on a wild look and he grabbed me. I screamed and screamed but no one came. When he unzipped his pants, I panicked. Without realizing it I grabbed the ceramic vase off the counter and hit him on the head. He fell to the floor and was still and quiet. After that, I ran from the house and out into the countryside."

"How did you survive?"

"I slept in an abandoned car I found off the beaten track. Eventually, I made it to Cheyenne and got a job, bussing tables in a fast-food restaurant. That's where I met Austin. He caught me eating leftover food from the table. He said if I'd come be his housekeeper and help with his horses, he'd protect me."

Now that the worst was over, she looked him in the eyes. "Of course, I didn't trust him but the chance to work with horses drew me in. I walked the entire way to the ranch. When he saw me coming up the track, he sat on the porch rocker and waited. He told me that we'd start first with the horses. After that, things just worked out."

Hayden cleared his throat. "You do understand that you did nothing wrong?"

"I know that now, but I struggled for a long time. Austin gave me a place to hide so I never really had to face my past."

"What happened to your parents?"

A bitter look suffused her face. "Nothing. It was my word against his and the tribal council said I just wanted attention. They told my parents I probably needed to see a counselor."

Hayden's face took on a ferocious look and his hands clenched into fists. "I'd like to punch all of them in the face. "Catching the wary look on Ginny's face his hand unfurled and came up to rest against her cheek. "Who do we need to see at the rez to get this settled?"

Ginny's gaze lowered to her hands in her lap. She took several moments before clearing her throat and speaking. "My parents. They're the ones who would have the old papers."

"Dammit." He lifted her chin and looked into her

eyes. "We don't have to do this. The only problem is the ranch title might not be clear. We need to check all possibilities before going to court. I'm sure Lancaster won't give up, so, we'll end up there. Can you, do it?"

"I don't know. I haven't seen either of them in over eight years. I have no idea if they're still together."

"Women who allow men to bully them don't change their actions. I'd say your mom is in the exact same place you left her and in the same predicament."

Ginny twisted her hands together but maintained eye contact. "What if he's still there? I don't know if I can face him."

Hayden stroked a finger around her cheek and lifted her chin. His head lowered and his lips met hers.

Ginny sucked in a quick breath before succumbing to his ardor. Her head began to spin with sensation. How could this man touch her so? Not just physically, but deep down touching her soul. She returned his passion with equal eagerness.

When she thought she could no longer breathe, he pulled back. "I'll leave it up to you. If you want, I'll go with you and stand by you. No one will hurt you again."

"I'd like to try." She took a deep breath. "It's best if we leave early in the morning before they have a chance to get out and about. I'll call a friend to let someone know I'm coming. She'll notify the gate that I'm her guest. That way we won't have to give my parents a heads up."

"I know this will be hard for you, but I also think it will be cathartic. You've let this scar your life for too long." He gave her another quick kiss and stood. "I need to get back to the stallion. I want to give the others a chance to eat while I take watch."

"Hayden?"

He turned back to her.

"I'm sorry I didn't stay for your celebration. I'm struggling with things right now. Congratulations on the arrival of Salvadore."

"Thanks, I best go." He exited the office.

Ginny wiped the tears from her eyes and stood. She also had work to do.

Chapter Twenty

Morning dawned crisp and clear. The coolness would burn off later in the day, leaving the normal afternoon heat. Ginny quickly showered and changed into her work clothes. The horses needed tending regardless of any other plans for the day. As she shoveled and raked, she tried to shake the fear away. It had an icy grip on her body. Her movements were jerky as she moved to grooming. She knew better than to approach a horse with fear in her heart, but it wouldn't go away. The horse picked up on it and was skittish. Taking a deep breath, she calmed the horse and herself.

"You're going to take the hide off that poor horse if you brush any harder." Ryan stood just behind her.

Startled, she dropped the brush. "Sorry, I've got stuff on my mind."

Ryan laughed and patted the chestnut on his neck. "Don't we all. The boss says you're to get ready. The rest of us can finish up."

"But—"

Hayden startled her with his interruption. "No buts."

"I need to—"

"The sooner we start, the sooner I'll be back here to help with the stallion. He's on twenty-four-hour watch."

"All right," she huffed. "I'll be ready in fifteen-minutes."

She turned quickly and ran for the house. Damn

Hayden Wilcoyt and his bossy ways. She was fuming by the time she reached her room. Ridding herself of the dusty clothes, she swiped the dust on her arms and face with a wet wipe. She patted her braid and put on her turquoise earrings and necklace. She chose her clothes carefully. Red was her favorite color, and it gave her courage. The sundress flounced just above her knees. Finally, she added lipstick and blush. Her reflection in the mirror told her she looked good, raising her confidence a notch. She was still scared but they wouldn't see it.

A half-hour later, they slowed down for the gate. The reservation was open to the public, but the tribal police kept close watch on visitors. Their aim was to slow crime and keep the tribal lands safe.

Hayden took his eyes off the gate and looked at her. "Are you all right?"

She smoothed her hand down the side of her skirt for the third time. "I'm fine, but I'll be glad when this is over. They might have a problem with you showing up unannounced."

Hayden nodded to the security officer as he drove forward. "Don't allow anyone to have power over you. If you go in, looking like you do now, you've lost the battle before we get there. Give me one of your 'Dam you to hell' looks."

Ginny's face crinkled into a smile.

Hayden flashed her a cocky grin. "Not that one. That's the one you save for me."

"You're a complete egotist. How do you stand to look at yourself in the mirror?"

Hayden laughed. "That's the ticket. Show your confidence."

She twisted her hands nervously. "I'm scared."

His hand shot out, grabbing hers. Rhythmically he rubbed circles on the back of her hand with his thumb.

Her heart squeezed. His gesture brought some measure of ease or—was that pleasure? He was such a mixture of hard and soft—though he'd die before admitting it. Not her bad ass, Ex-Navy SEAL now hard-working rancher. Her body tightened at the thought. When had he become her anything? A steal door slammed shut on the thought. He wasn't hers and… would he ever be?

When Hayden came to the four-way stop and her attention was drawn to her surroundings. Things had grown. There was a grocery now and a small bank. The amount of poverty was the same. Little squat houses with old cars and appliances in the yards. Part of her had missed this. The other part wanted to know what the hell she was doing here. "Turn left at the corner."

A little white church sat on the right. The grass was immaculate, and the building looked freshly painted. *Priorities,* she thought. Some things came before yards and houses. "Take a right at the next stop sign and the house is the third one on the left."

As Hayden pulled into the driveway, Ginny studied the house where she'd grown up. It was painted the same faded, yellow, and looked like it needed a new roof. Hell, it had needed a roof when *she'd* lived there. Black shutters trimmed the windows and the door had been painted turquoise. Flowers bloomed among the edges of the rocked bed. Her mother must have taken up gardening. In the old days she'd spent the days doing housework and watching her soaps. Her eye caught a twitch of the front room curtain. Her gut twisted.

Hayden came around to open her door. Leaning in, he whispered. "You've got this."

Ginny gave him a quick smile as she stood and closed the car door. There was no going back. She had to face this. The door opened before she knocked. An older version of her mother stood in the doorway, smiling. Then a pair of arms wrapped around her, and the smell of jasmine filled her senses. It had always been her mother's favorite. She stood stiffly as her mother babbled. This wasn't the reception she expected to receive. "Hello, Mother." Her words sounded hollow and a bit shaky. She cleared her throat and introduced Hayden. "Mom, this is Hayden Wilcoyt. He's the new owner of the ranch."

Hayden shook the woman's hand. "Nice to meet you, Mrs. Hampton."

Ginny watched her mother beam at Hayden. She'd never seen her so happy. "Please sit." Her mother indicated the comfy-looking sofa.

Ginny continued to watch her mother. She'd never seen her smile and talk so openly. "We're not here on a social visit. I need to ask you some questions." Her voice strengthened, sounding firm and a little brittle.

"Certainly, Gin.

She was unprepared for the nickname. Memories flooded her mind. Tinsel-covered Christmas trees, homemade cookies. She yanked her mind back to the present. "Where is Jack?" She couldn't bear to call him father.

Her mother's smile faded, and her gaze dropped to her lap. "He's been charged with statutory rape and is in prison, pending the trial."

Anger rose in Ginny's chest. She'd told people about

him for years and an innocent had to suffer before they caught him. "I told you about him and you wouldn't listen. The day I left, he tried to rape me." Her voice rose and she leaned forward. "I went through hell, and you said nothing. Why did you let it happen?"

Hayden wrapped an arm around her shoulders. The small measure of comfort gave her strength. She swiped the tears from her cheeks and once more waited for an answer to the question that had plagued her throughout her life. Why would a woman allow a husband to abuse their daughter?

"He hated you. He threatened to break your arms and hurt you in so many ways." Her mother paused, took a breath. "Jack Hampton isn't your father. Your birth father died while I was still carrying you. I was lost and frightened. At seventeen, I was a pregnant widow with no job. He offered to marry me, and I jumped at the chance to have a home and husband."

"Not my father?' The words squeaked past a throat now gone dry. "Then who—

"That doesn't matter now. I made bad choices and you suffered because of them. You didn't deserve the abuse and I should have stood up to him and gotten a divorce."

"You're dammed right you should have," Ginny yelled. "I looked to you to save me, but you ignored me. Do you understand that I cried each night as I cringed beneath the covers? I never knew when he'd show up. I—I needed you and you weren't there."

A sudden silence fell between the two women and Hayden cleared his throat. "Mrs. Hampton, the matter between your daughter and you won't be settled in a day. We came here today to ask you some questions. Do you feel up to it?"

"Yes, I can answer some questions. What do you need to know?"

Ginny pulled herself together and spoke up. "There's a rumor going around town saying my grandmother was at one time married to Austin Wilcoyt. Is there truth to this?"

Ginny's mother still looked at her clasped hands. "She never spoke of it, but others did. They say she married him when she was very young in our joining ceremony. Unlike the white man's marriage, there were no formal vows. It is said that years later she returned home to her people, and no one spoke of the marriage."

"Was there any paperwork describing the marriage? We need to clear up a question about Austin's property."

"I'm not sure. That was a very long time ago."

"Aren't there some of her things still in your possession?" As she waited for an answer, Ginny took a deep breath and tried to calm herself. Hayden leaned forward as if willing the woman to hurry with her answer.

"I do have a few things left in the attic," her mother said. "We could check there."

Ginny had never seen any of these things and was excited to discover the things that had been forgotten. "Could we, please? I'd love to see some of my history."

Suddenly Ginny's mother looked unsure. "I can't promise anything."

Ginny was quick to reassure her. "I understand but I'd still like to see her things."

Moments later, at her mother's direction, Hayden pulled down a set of stairs that led to the attic. Ginny followed her mother up the steps with nervous anticipation. It wasn't the marriage information but the historical meaning of her grandmother's things which caused her heart to beat faster. She quelled her irritation as her mother paused over box after box of useless stuff. Then she heard an exclamation coming from the farthest corner of the attic. "This is it."

"What is it? Ginny raced over to her mother.

"It's a box and an old basket filled with things. I'll go down so your young man can come carry this down."

Ginny ignored the 'your young man' comment and hurried her mother to the stairs. Soon, Hayden's head appeared at the head of the stairs. She circled both arms around him and gave him a hug. She was so excited.

Hayden squeezed back and then stepped back. "You take the basket and I'll get the box."

Downstairs they placed the items on the coffee table. Ginny gently touched the old basket, admiring the workmanship. Some of the patterns were very old, some of figures dancing, others gathering corn. She removed the top and set it aside. Her eyes widened at the old bead necklaces, leather pouches and a woven shawl. "I can't believe these have survived." She looked at Hayden, whose eyes were glued to the box before him. It was filled with papers.

"These look more modern," he said.

"There was no official license like today. It would have been described as an event in the community and definitely not written on regular paper."

She picked up a leather pouch and opened it. Inside was a sheepskin rolled around a spindle. She unrolled it with nervous fingers. Once open, the skin showed rows of pictures, roughly drawn. It told the story of the death of a warrior. "It would look something like this." She rerolled the skin and carefully put it back in its pouch.

Hayden set the box aside and watched as she opened the next pouch.

A chunky turquoise and silver necklace fell into her hand. She couldn't stop the gasp of pleasure from escaping. All these wonderful treasures had been ignored for decades. She looked at her mother. "Could we borrow these things and go through them later? Hayden must return to the ranch to help with a new stallion."

"You may have them. These things belong to you. I kept them hidden upstairs to keep your father—Jack—from selling them."

"Are you sure? Historically these are priceless and monetarily worth quite a bit."

"I'm sure they will be kept safe in your hands."

Ginny looked at her mother closely. She saw the age lines and signs of a hard life. Closer still, she saw the sadness in her chocolate brown eyes. She didn't know if she could ever forgive her, but she might someday come to understand her motives. "Thank you. I will treasure them and keep them safe for my daughter one day."

Hayden placed the box and basket behind the truck seat and settled in. "Are you okay? he asked as she buckled up.

"I've got a lot to think about and my brain is fried right now."

He started the engine. "Let's go home then."

Ginny sighed as she leaned back into the seat. Home sounded good. "Yes, let's."

Chapter Twenty-One

Hayden wiped sweat from his forehead with the back of his hand. The heat was intolerable, and the air smelled of a storm. He and the other men stayed busy working with the stallion while waiting for the vet to arrive. The animal was magnificent. From the tuft of curly hair between his ears to the tip of his braided tail, Salvadore was a quivering mass of coiled muscle. The two men who had accompanied the stallion were adept at getting the horse to behave. Hayden hoped his people would quickly learn the methods from them.

"Watch for his hind legs," the groom shouted to Ryan.

He motioned to the groom. It was his time to maneuver the horse into and out of the stall. It was a daunting prospect. He took the reins and spoke softly to the horse. Salvadore nickered a response. With the training crop in one hand and the reins in the other, Hayden tapped the inside of the horses back legs and gave the command. "Back."

The horse hesitated, then began to inch backward. Hayden was elated. Something was going right for once. The breeze brought the smell of the impending storm to the horse, and he lunged forward. Caught off guard, Hayden struggled to stay on his feet as the horse crashed into him.

So much for things going right. Pushing against the

broad chest of the horse, he planted his feet and regained his balance. He breathed a sigh of relief when the vet's van pulled in and stopped. "Take a break, everyone. We'll let Dr. Sanderson get acquainted with Salvadore."

The vet walked over to the group of men. "Let me see this wonder horse."

Hayden laughed. "All right, Edith. This is Salvadore. He's a bit skittish with the storm brewing."

Edith ran her hands down the stallion's neck and began her exam.

Hayden handed the reins to the groom and walked toward the house. The cool interior was heaven compared to outside. "Noel, have you seen Ginny?"

"Today's grocery day, señor. She should be back in a little bit. I just fixed fresh lemonade. Would you like a glass?"

"You're a goddess." He took the glass she poured and drank it down, then headed for the office. The past few days had been busy, and the room had been transformed. It was now a true office with a Murphy bed for extra guests. He admired the old desk all cleaned up and sat in his new ergonomic chair. He was beginning to worry about Ginny. They had barely spoken since returning from the reservation. She'd had plenty of time to go through the things from her mother. Either she'd found something and was upset or not found something and was afraid to tell him. Either way, she was being far too quiet.

****

Ginny closed her purse and placed the tip on the table. The waitress was new to Maggie's so she'd left a little extra. Rhonda, her regular waitress had moved away to college. She sighed at the town's loss of another talented youth. As she stood, she realized the diner was unusually quiet. Looking around, she saw everyone staring at her. What was their problem? Suddenly embarrassed, she looked down at her shirt to see if she'd spilled something.

Seeing nothing, she stood straighter and stared back at the rude diners. The look she gave said more than 'mind your business.' It said, 'I'm not the one with the problem.' The bell jangled as she left Maggie's. It didn't sound near as cheerful as when she'd entered.

Minutes later, she pulled into the parking lot of Nate's Grocery. It was crowded so she had to drive around to find a parking spot. As she walked in, groups of people stopped talking and stared at her. Ignoring them, she started at the top of her list and pushed her cart down the aisles. On the salad isle she ran into her lawyer, Mr. Benson.

"Morning, Ginny. Lots of buzz in town today."

Ginny picked up a bag of salad mix and dropped it into the cart. "I've noticed. What's the deal?"

"You're the deal. There's a rumor going around that you might have a claim on the ranch."

She selected some carrots and tomatoes. "That rumor has been around for years. Why the sudden interest now?"

Mr. Benson picked up a head of lettuce. "Now, there is another player involved. Hayden Wilcoyt might lose the ranch to you."

Ginny's heart pounded. It's what she'd wanted. She could call the shots and make a go of it. "Let's just wait and see. I'm sorry, I have to buy these groceries and get home."

"Sure. Will I see you at the Wylder County Horse

Show?"

Ginny sucked in a quick breath. The death of the foal was still too hurtful to think about. She took a moment then answered. "It depends. I'm sure you've heard of the trouble we've been having. We may need to watch the ranch.

The thought of Hayden losing the ranch brought a pall to the vivid picture she had imagined. No matter what the rumors, Austin had wanted Hayden to inherit the ranch. He had a dream for the ranch. One that she could support. She would enjoy building a new business for the ranch but—she couldn't do it alone. She didn't have the overwhelming drive to make his dream come true. Shaking her head to clear her thoughts, she quickly picked up the rest of the items on her list.

An hour later, Ginny pulled up at the house and stopped. In seconds, Hayden was outside to help carry things in. "Did you have a nice trip?"

She avoided looking at him "Sort of. I had time enough to pick up a few personals and a quick lunch. People were staring at me in the cafe. It was the strangest thing. I gave them a look and left."

"I'd like to see that look. We can add it to the others in your repertoire."

She laughed and went back to the truck for another load.

"This looks like enough food for an army."

"You may have noticed; we have three times the number of people staying here.

He placed the last load of groceries on the counter. "I do recall stepping over quite a few pairs of boots. Why don't you come into the office? I have some questions."

"Am I in trouble again?" Her voice came out half

joking, half challenging.

He settled into the chair, pointing to the other comfy chair that now sat beside the desk.

Ginny sat and spoke before he could utter a sound. " Austin would cringe if he could see his office now."

"I know the place has undergone some changes and that makes you feel uncomfortable, but things had to change for this operation to turn around. Are you all right with the alterations to the house?"

"I don't spend a lot of time inside, so I don't mind them. The changes with the horses are more difficult to accept. I was used to doing things my own way. I had complete autonomy. Things are a little different in that category."

"That's more words than you've spoken to me in a week. What's wrong?"

"Nothing is wrong. I've been quiet because of the things from my mother's. I did find a leather pouch containing a sheepskin, speaking about the marriage. Unfortunately, it doesn't have Austin's name in it. We need to show it to the lawyer and see what he says."

"Anything else?"

"Some exquisite jewelry, some pressed flowers, and a few more sheepskins. I'll need to check with a museum to find out more about them."

"Then why the avoidance?"

She looked down at her lap and then up at him. "I suppose I'm embarrassed. You heard all my dirty secrets. I just hate to think you might treat me differently now."

"You did nothing wrong. If anything, I admire you for not letting it defeat you."

The phone interrupted their conversation.

"Yes? I'll be right there." He put the phone down and

looked at Ginny. "I've got to see Edith before she leaves. There's still another matter I want to discuss. Can we meet after supper?

Ginny gave him a guarded look. "Sure."

Hayden picked up his hat and they left together.

Chapter Twenty-Two

Two days later, Ginny sat on a bale of hay, oiling tack. The extra help Hayden brought in from the local agricultural school allowed them catch up on long overdue tasks. The tack had been ignored for a long time. The familiar smell of the oil was comforting. The mindless chore allowed her time to think. She had enough to think about. Hayden had asked her to take over the books. She would do them daily, and then have a professional check them monthly. It wasn't like she hadn't done it before, but on a large scale like the new breeding business—it was a little scary.

"Hey, Ginny." Monte pulled a bale of hay over and sat across from her.

"How did you pull yourself away from Salvadore?" Ginny asked with a grin.

Monte grabbed a bridle and a rag. "I've worked with the stallion on my father's ranch. Hayden needs to get experience with him without me standing watch."

"Poor Hayden," Ginny teased, then sobered. "He's had so much thrown at him at once."

"Don't go feeling sorry for him. I've seen all the things he can do. This is easy compared to the missions we went on."

"He doesn't say much about them or anything he did with the SEALs."

Monte continued to rub oil into the bridle. "Rightly

so. Our missions are classified. What's bugging you about it?"

Ginny took a moment to gather her thoughts and chose her words carefully. "When he first arrived, he was thrown from his spooked horse and had a flashback. I went to help, and he grabbed me. He didn't recognize me. Later, he said that if he'd had his knife, I'd be dead. Is that the norm for people who do your kind of work?"

Monte worked the bridle several seconds before answering. "We all handle the horror in different ways. Some men drink to forget; others shut everyone out. Some bury their anguish deep down and only release it when affected by trauma. Sounds like Hayden is in that category. Regardless of what he said, I doubt he would hurt you. His moral code is so strong, it would overcome his instinct to kill."

"How can you be sure?"

"Hayden is like a brother to me. The teams forge bonds that last a lifetime. I know him. I've trusted my life to him countless times. I'd do it again in a heartbeat. Sounds like you have problems trusting men. Hayden is one man you can trust." He raised a brow but said nothing more.

Ginny's heart raced. Had Hayden shared her story with Monte? No, he would never share her private trauma. Monte was just a perceptive man. "It's not just men. I have trouble with people in general. Give me a horse any day. At least when they show emotions, they're honest."

Monte laughed. "Sometimes their tantrums can get dangerous. He dropped the bridle and checked his watch. "When was the last time you went out on the town?"

Ginny gave him a hard look. "What's that got to do

with things?"

"I find it helps settle all those annoying thoughts about important stuff. Sometimes you need to let off steam. Is there a place in town or do we need to go into the city?" He took the tack from her hands.

Ginny made a grab for the leather. "There's too much work to do."

"It'll be here when we get back."

"Have you forgotten about people shooting and trying to kill our horses?

He held the piece out of her reach. "There are enough people around. We tough guys will draw straws to see who stays."

"You're serious?"

"Yeah, I am. And Hayden and I will both draw long straws."

"How are you going to manage that?"

Monte sprang from the hay and reached a hand to Ginny. That's easy. I'll be holding the straws. Now get dolled up."

Ginny couldn't help smiling. "What will the boss have to say about this?"

"He'll probably say something along the lines of I have shit for brains. Then, he'll jump on board. Red is his favorite color by the way."

She began to feel giddy with the thought of dressing up for Hayden. "Are you playing matchmaker?"

"Never. I'll tell the others while you get a head start."

Ginny dropped his hand and swung away. Five minutes later she was in the shower.

****

Hayden was pissed at Monte for organizing this

outing without consulting him. Though to be honest, they were equal partners, and everyone *did* need a break. He tuned out the old country ballad on the radio—Ginny had won the coin toss again—and concentrated on the road. Anything that might happen wouldn't depend upon his presence. They couldn't get too relaxed. The shooter was still out there and waiting for something to happen was stretching everyone's nerves.

Her fragrance, something floral with a little spice, penetrated his thoughts. Dressed in black skintight pants with silver studs running down the legs, she made a fetching distraction. The off shoulder red crop-top made his heart beat a little faster.

"Are you going to be mad all night?"

He stopped at the road leading into town. "I'm not mad, just a little peeved. I should have been consulted before everyone quit work early and headed for the showers."

"You and Monte are partners. There are going to be times he makes decisions without you. Admit it. Everyone needs a break."

Hayden turned onto the pavement and shot her a grin. "I admit that things have been tense. Tonight, should ease some of the strain."

Minutes later, he pulled into a parking spot in front of the Silver Buckle bar. The smell of grilled steaks greeted his nose as he stepped from the truck. His stomach growled in anticipation. As he helped Ginny down from the truck, his arm brushed against her bare midriff. His manhood tightened. Thoughts of food fled his mind as he wondered if her tanned skin would taste as silky as it looked.

Ginny stepped back and came up against his chest.

"You clean up pretty good, cowboy. I hardly recognize you without the jeans and kerchief."

Hayden sucked in his breath at her touch. He wanted to pull her into his arms and kiss every inch of her body. "You've got a bit of shine and sparkle, too." He took her elbow to move her away from the empty parking spot.

"Here's the rest of the gang." Ginny stepped up on the curb as the SUV parked beside them.

Adam moved from behind the wheel and Peyton exited the passenger door. Ryan, his wife, Becky, and Monte got out the back. There was an air of festivity as everyone moved inside the bar. For a small-town establishment, the Silver Buckle was a little upscale. It offered everyone a nice place to eat without having to go into Cheyenne. Country music came from a juke box and couples were dancing on the small, raised platform. Hayden looked forward to holding Ginny snug against his body as they moved to the music.

Ryan pulled out a seat for his wife as the others found chairs around the table. "I can't remember the last time we went out for some fun."

Peyton slapped Ryan on the back. "We could tell, buddy."

Hayden seated Ginny and caught the attention of a server. "Beers for the guys and white wine for the ladies. We'll look at a menu while we wait for drinks."

"I'm glad I like white wine." Ginny said.

"Sorry about that," Hayden sat. "There's a crowd tonight and I didn't want to wait too long. We'll order whatever you like next time."

"Sounds good," Becky chimed in.

Hayden noticed Ginny, tapping her finger to the beat of the song. "Would you like to dance?"

She flashed him a brilliant smile. "I thought you'd never ask."

He took her hand, leading her out onto the floor. Ryan and Becky were right behind them. As they stepped onto the floor, the lively tune ended. When the music restarted, he recognized the singer. The guitar music perfectly complimented the man's voice and a hush fell over the crowd. With her hand in his and an arm around her back, Ginny settled into his embrace. It was heavenly. Her curves nestled to his hard muscles. As they swayed to the music, Ginny rubbed little circles on his shoulders. Her touch inflamed him.

She leaned back and looked up into his face. "This is nice."

He breathed in her scent as he stared at her mouth. All he had to do was bend his head and he could claim those luscious lips. Her eyes sparkled up at him with excitement. She must have read his mind because she leaned back putting a little space between them.

Ginny gave him a seductive smile that promised more than kisses. "Later, cowboy."

His gut tightened when her smile brightened, and she moved closer. Irritation came with a tap on his shoulder. He wouldn't put it past one of his buddies to try and cut in. He wasn't about to share. Possessiveness tightened his grip on Ginny's lithe form.

The annoying tap came again. He scowled as he turned to rebuke his friend. It wasn't either of his friends, but Jeff who stood behind him. A cocky grin on his face, Jeff had the air of a man who had imbibed too liberally for his own good. Before the jerk could speak, Hayden grabbed a fistful of Jeff's shirt and lifted him from the floor.

"Hey, man. I just want a dance," Jeff yelled.

The crowd quietened and all eyes turned their way.

Ginny tugged on his arm. "Let him go. You're making a scene."

Hayden ignored her urgent plea and continued to hold Jeff. "I told you not to ever go near her again."

"Are you making her decisions for her, now?"

Ginny pulled harder on Hayden's arm. "Shut up, Jeff. You're only making matters worse."

He slowly let Jeff back down. Just as he turned toward Ginny, Jeff punched him. The blow caught him on the side of the jaw and slid away. He retaliated with a gut punch, full force.

Jeff fell backward and the other dancers hopped off the stage. After catching his breath, he screamed, "Call the sheriff. I want this man arrested for assault."

Adam and Peyton joined Hayden and Ginny on the stage. "It was self-defense. He hit Hayden first," Adam informed the crowd gathered around the dance floor.

A siren sounded. And it was close. Hayden took Ginny's arm to lead her off the dance floor. She snatched her arm back and rushed ahead of him. When he reached the chairs, the front door opened, and Sheriff Bannister walked in. "What's going on here? I had a call about a fight."

The owner of the bar set down his tray and walked to the center of the room. "Nothing much—just a couple of punches. Nobody's hurt."

"Arrest him, sheriff. He assaulted me," Jeff whined from the floor.

"Who assaulted you?"

Hayden stood. "That would be me. I hit him after he sucker-punched me."

"Mr. Wilcoyt, you've only been in town a few times and yet you stand out in a crowd. Why did you really hit him?"

Hayden cursed under his breath. He hadn't even started his beer and the sheriff was painting him as a troublemaker. "I don't look for trouble, but it seems to follow me. Jeff was fired from the ranch for manhandling Ginny. I told him not to come near her again. Tonight, he tried to cut in when she and I were dancing, I elevated him by the shirt. After I put him down, he punched me when I turned away. I returned the punch."

"That's all true, sheriff," the owner said.

"Well then," Bannister said, hitching up his belt. "Let me have a little chat with Jeff. Do you want to press charges, Mr. Wilcoyt?"

"Only if he causes more trouble. I'd really like to eat and enjoy the evening with my friends."

"I'll get back to you if I have more questions. Enjoy your meal."

Hayden sighed. He could tell with one look at Ginny, he wouldn't be enjoying the evening she'd alluded to. Her eyes sparked with anger. He pulled out his chair and looked around the table. "I hope everyone can put these events aside and enjoy the rest of our night out."

The waiter arrived with their beer and wine. His had a note attached. It read, '*This one is on me. Thanks.*' He looked over at the bar and received a slight nod from the owner. He acknowledged the nod with one of his own, then took a long pull on his beer. The waiter took their orders and the group cheered up—except for Ginny. She was breathing fire and sending cutting looks at him.

"How are the mustangs doing, Ginny?" Monte

asked.

At first, she said nothing, then said, "The Appaloosa is almost ready to receive a saddle. It took a while for her to accept a blanket."

Monte leaned back as the server placed bread and honey flavored butter on the table. "When will they be ready to breed?"

Hayden took a roll and butter as he watched Ginny from beneath hooded lids. As soon as Monte mentioned the horses, her back relaxed and her fingers eased her fork from a death grip. Why couldn't she be as relaxed with him? She must still be angry about Jeff. What was he supposed to have done? Allow the jerk to put his hands on Ginny? Hell, no. Not in this lifetime.

Ginny's face took on a rosy hue. "Some of the *when* depends on how prepared you guys are. Are you ready for pregnant mares? We still need to ramp up the barns and set up data collecting procedures."

"We're having horses not computers," Hayden cut in. His phone rang before he could finish his thought. He stepped away from the table before answering the phone. "Cooper? What's up?"

"There's a fire near the barns. We need help p.d.q."

Hayden dropped his phone in his pocket while Cooper was still talking. "Everyone, get to the car. We have to leave, now. He dropped a bill on the table and made for his truck.

Ginny got the door open and was inside the vehicle before Hayden. "What's wrong?"

"Call the fire department, if this place has one, and the sheriff. Again. We've got a fire at the ranch near the barns."

"The horses!"

"Call, now!" He raced from the parking spot like a bullet fired from a rifle. The tires shrieked as he hit the gas.

Ginny grabbed the 'chicken bar' and held on. "You're going to get us killed. Slow down."

"I'll slow down when we get there. When you finish those calls, make another call to Monte. They need a heads up before we get there.

****

The glow on the horizon made Hayden's heart miss a beat. Ginny grabbed his hand and squeezed. Her silence was unusual enough to express the seriousness of the situation. He jammed on brakes in front of the house. Slamming the door to the truck, he ran toward the burning stable. Halfway there, Cooper stopped him and thrust a bucket into his hands.

"What about the horses?" Hayden yelled over the sounds of screaming animals.

"We put most of them in the arena. We needed more men to help get them into the far paddock."

The SUV stopped beside the house. Everyone piled out and ran toward the barn.

Hayden started spouting orders. "Ryan, get around back. Use the hose to wet down the grass and barn." Hayden filled his bucket with water and handed it to Noelle's father. "Peyton, you and Adam get to the workhorse barn and saddle up several horses. We're going to need them to get the horses to the far paddock"

Ginny started toward the arena. "I'll go try to calm the arena horses. They'll be scared to death."

"Ginny, wait. Take Becky with you. She can hold the paddock gate when we push the horses through. Are you okay with that?" Hayden gave Becky an encouraging smile.

"Don't worry. I'll be fine." She took off after Ginny.

Monte pressed a hand to Hayden's shoulder. "What about me?"

"We'll get the stallion and tie him up close to the house. I want him as far away from the barns as possible.

"I understand the need, but isn't it kind of risky?" Monte pulled a set of gloves from his pocket.

Hayden swiped sweat from his brow, looking up at the sound of a siren. "It's the best we can do."

The sheriff's car pulled in beside the SUV. An old-fashioned fire truck passed the sheriff's unit, stopping close to the barn. Six men slipped from the cab and headed for the equipment. Hayden's lip quirked up a little as he saw the bar owner step from the truck and slip a captain's helmet on his head. Again, he gave the man a nod, then headed toward the stud barn.

Salvadore could be heard pounding the stall gate over all the noise and chaos. Thankfully, there was very little smoke in the barn. At least they didn't have to worry about smoke inhalation. Monte approached the gate, whispering to the animal as he moved closer. The horse reared onto his hind legs, pounding the gate with his front legs. Monte paused, waiting for the animal to calm.

"Unfortunately, we don't have time to baby him. Let's get a rope on him before we get much closer." Hayden stepped forward with the lasso and caught the horse on first try.

"You're getting good at this cowboy thing." Monte grabbed another rope and dropped it over the animal's head. When the horse reared again, Hayden pulled on the rope which stopped the horse from pounding the gate.

"This would be easier if we had horses," said Monte.

Together they got the gate open and the horse out of the stall. Smelling freedom from the barn, the horse surged forward, knocking Monte off his feet.

"Get the rope," Hayden called as he dug in his boot heels and plowed through the dirt. The horse dragged him toward the door. He felt the burn on his hands as he held tight to the rope.

Monte stood and tightened the rope. The horse stopped and they walked him outside. Once again, Salvadore tried to take off. The efforts of the two men were rewarded as the horse came to a stop, pawing the ground.

Adam handed Trigger's reins to him. He mounted, tying the rope to the saddle horn. Monte got on one of the other horses and they walked the horse toward the back of the house. The oak tree stood broad and sturdy by the private cemetery. Hayden thought it poetic justice as he tied his rope around the tree. Angus had always wanted a prize stallion to build a herd. Now, here stood Salvadore.

"We best get back," Monte said.

An hour later, the blaze was out with minimal damage to the barn. The horses were in the far paddock with two men riding the perimeter quietening the animals. The men brought in fans to blow any vestige of smoke from the barn. Now, they needed to bring the horse back to his stall. Hayden grabbed a pitchfork and put in new hay.

"We'll get him," Cooper said. He and Adam rode off to the house.

Less than two minutes later, they thundered to a stop in front of Hayden.

"Where's the stallion?" Hayden asked quickly. Part of him knew the answer and his gut tightened.

"He's gone," Adam said. "The ropes were cut."

"Dammit to hell. He was here the entire time, just waiting for us to move the horse."

"I'll get in touch with Mustang Joe," Monte said. "I don't know what he can do tonight but it's best to cover all our bases."

Hayden swallowed hard. All his dreams were going to Hell in a hand basket. He'd worked so hard, invested his life savings, and now with a little flame, it could all be gone. The horse was insured but that did not matter. The horse mattered.

"We'll get him back," Monte interrupted his pity party. "Wherever he runs he'll be on your land. We just have to get a search party together."

Hayden straightened his shoulders. "You're right. We'll have Mustang take a look, then everyone gets a few hours' sleep. We'll be up before dawn to search."

Cooper stepped from behind the house. "Adam, Peyton and I will take watch. We'll shoot first and not ask any questions."

Hayden smiled for the first time since receiving the call. "Just don't shoot the damn horse."

"Got it, boss.

Hayden turned to go inside and came face to face with Ginny. "Sorry about our evening out."

She placed a palm against his chest. "I'm so sorry about Salvadore. Most horses don't go running off into the unknown. He'll be close by."

"The ropes were cut. They could have taken him."

"They didn't bring a truck. We would have heard them. Salvadore isn't too keen on getting into a trailer."

Hayden took her hand and placed a kiss upon her palm. "We could play what ifs all night. The truth is, we have to wait until tomorrow. You go in and get your shower. I need to think for a few minutes."

"Don't think too hard. You'll start blaming yourself when you couldn't have stopped it. This was a well-planned attack."

Hayden pulled her in for a swift kiss. "Goodnight. I'll see you at dawn."

****

Dawn came early. Everyone scarfed down Noel's bacon biscuits with gusto, then headed outside. As Hayden stepped onto the porch, Ryan and Ginny brought Trigger and four other horses out of the barn. Mustang Joe's truck and horse trailer were parked near the barn, announcing his arrival. Mustang, Ginny, and Hayden's four friends would go on the search. Ryan and the others would stay and get the cleanup from the fire started.

"Mustang, we'll follow your lead. Have you checked out the tracks?"

"There are plenty of tracks. At least two riders and Salvadore. I followed them up toward the lake but lost the trail where it gets rocky. We might need to split up to cover that whole area." Mustang mounted his horse along with the others.

Hayden looked at the group. "Everyone should be armed and with a partner. Ginny, you know the area so you're with me and Peyton. Mustang, you take Monte, Cooper and Adam. Keep your radios tuned to channel two." He grabbed Trigger's reins and hoisted himself into the saddle.

"Any signs of trucks or trailers?" Mustang asked.

"No. They're on horseback. Even with the delay,

they should still be on your land."

"Good. Let's go."

Mustang took the lead as they headed for Teardrop Lake. Once there, they pulled up and waited as Mustang examined the ground. "See where the rocky part starts. I can't pick up their tracks from here."

Hayden dismounted and observed the tracks. "All right. The two groups will separate and spread out.

Ginny edged her horse forward. "Which way do you want us to go, Joe?"

"You take the Northeast corner and I'll take the flats. If we don't find anything, meet back here in two hours."

Hayden remounted and followed Ginny to the other side of the lake. Keeping watch on the surroundings, he listened carefully, hoping to hear the stallion. It was too quiet. A few birds, the rustle of leaves and the jangle of the tack on the horses. How could a horse as big as Salvadore disappear on this property? Yes, it was four thousand acres, but wouldn't a new horse want to stay close to what he knew? Of course, the fire may have scared him so much he kept moving away from the barn.

Ginny pulled up and dismounted. There was a muddy patch on the edge of the pathway.

"Found something? he called.

Ginny touched the muddy area with her hand. "There's a hoof print and it's large. It could be him."

"Should we radio Mustang?"

"Not yet. Let's see if we see anything more."

Hayden studied her face as she remounted. "What's got that worried look on your face?"

"Austin's property ends soon. They could have had a truck and trailer on the adjacent property."

"Once he's in a trailer, he could be anywhere.

Dammit we've got to find him."

Peyton rode up beside Ginny. Should we split up? We could cover more ground faster. We've got GPSS and radios. We should be safe enough."

Hayden weighed Peyton's comments. "No. I don't like it. Too much has happened for us to disregard safety." He pulled out his radio and thumbed the call button. "Do you hear me, Monte?"

Loud and clear. Have you found something?

"We've found a single track. It could be Salvadore. We're getting close to the property line. Could be they had a truck and trailer on the next property."

We'll come meet you. You might need backup.

"Got that." Hayden put the radio away. He turned to Ginny. "What's your suggestion?"

"We should go on. They have hours of time ahead of us. Mustang will take a shortcut and be close behind."

"All right. Let's go. If they're still there, we'll stay low and wait on the others." He nudged Trigger and sped forward.

Fifteen minutes later, Ginny stopped again. Once more she got down and checked for tracks. She pointed to the ground, brushing away a leaf. "There's definitely two riders with the stallion. Looks like he gave them a little trouble here." Her voice dropped. "There something that looks like blood. Not much, but enough to say someone's hurt."

Hayden jumped down and stared at the red splotches. It was blood, no question. His stomach tightened as his hands clenched. If they'd hurt Salvadore—his mind couldn't think of a just punishment. Bare-fisted beating or hanging came to mind. Nothing legal. Hoofbeats came from behind them. From around the bend, Mustang and the others trotted up.

Immediately, Mustang was down beside Ginny, checking the tracks. "These are only a few hours old. They must have rested for a couple of hours. The blood could be horse or man. There's not enough to tell if it's a major wound or just a scratch."

"Good. We'll move on," Hayden said. "Now that we're all together, we can take them if they've stopped."

Monte moved beside Hayden. "We're all armed. It's a possibility they are too. If bullets fly, the horse could get hit."

"What do you suggest?"

"We should only fire if absolutely necessary and then away from the horse."

Hayden nodded his head. "That's sound advice. But what if they use the horse as a shield?"

Monte laughed. "We're shit out of luck."

Hayden patted Monte's shoulder. "I've got an idea. Let's use some SEAL team tactics. Let Ginny and Joe keep moving slowly toward the target while the rest of us branch out and sneak up on them from the sides. Wait for about ten minutes before you move on."

"Sounds like a plan," Mustang said.

"But—"

"No buts, Ginny. We're trained for this kind of maneuver. Promise me you'll stay with your uncle."

Hayden watched the anger, disgruntlement and then acceptance cross her face. Would she ever trust him? He wanted to take her into his arms and explain things completely. There wasn't time. They had to move quickly if they had any hope of saving the stallion.

"I promise."

From the visual arrows she shot in his direction, he

was certain there would be retribution. When had things been any different? He made eye contact with each of the men and then disappeared into the woods.

Quiet surrounded him. The woods weren't thick but there was plenty of cover. With ease he stealthily moved though the underbrush. He couldn't hear them but knew the approximate location of each of his men. They'd done this on numerous missions. In a way it was a similar scenario. A high-profile hostage taken for ransom with the SEALs planning and carrying out a daring rescue. He'd give anything for the intel on the kidnappers. Were they smart, trained, or paid lackeys? He hoped for the latter.

Without a personal stake in the crime, the culprits would be less likely to put up a fight. A panicked scream came from an animal up ahead. Hayden slowed and neared the clearing. They'd been right to worry. There was the truck and trailer. The two men were having difficulty getting the stallion into the trailer. He remembered it had taken a team to get the animal out when he'd first arrived. Salvadore looked okay, better perhaps than his handlers.

"You said this would be a piece of cake," Jeffrey McCallister whined.

A small-framed man answered. "It was the boss' idea. Don't blame me."

"Yeah, but I had the idea of the truck and trailer," Jeffrey whined. "He only wanted us to let the stallion go. We'll make a fortune selling this horse."

Hayden clenched his fists, wishing they were around McCallister's neck. No wonder the enemy was so well informed. He must have made bail and raced to the ranch to help his friend. He'd bet anything the other man was

Ginny's missing ranch hand, Rick. With a click to his radio, he let the others know he was ready. He waited for everyone to get in position before making his move. He moved to the edge of the clearing and stood up. The two men were concentrating their efforts and attention on Salvadore.

"You gentlemen mind telling me what you're doing with my horse?"

Jeff let go his rope and ran toward the cab of the truck.

He made it about three steps before Hayden tackled him. Monte and the others took the stranger down with ease. Salvadore reared and took off down the trail. Jeff continued to struggle, and Hayden took the opportunity to release some pent-up tension. His fist met Jeff's jaw with a loud, satisfying crack.

"That should hold him for a little while," Cooper said. He picked up the rope that Jeff had dropped.

"Somehow, I get the feeling this isn't over," Peyton said.

Hayden pulled out his phone. "Not by a long shot. Anyone got any reception?"

"I brought the SAT phone," Cooper said and handed the phone to Hayden. "I plugged the sheriff's number into the phone last week."

"Thanks, it's time to call in the heavyweights."

"Yes, this is Hayden Wilcoyt. I need to speak to Sheriff Bannister. Tell him I've caught the people who stole my horse. He can meet us at the edge of my property and parcel three which adjoins my land." He punched the button cutting off the call.

He looked up as Mustang and Ginny came into the clearing. Both held a rope attached to Salvadore. "You guys were supposed to catch the horse, not let him loose," Ginny said with a big smile on her face.

"It's good to see you've caught him. We got the bad guys."

Ginny gasped. "Jeff. Is he all right? I can't believe he was behind all this."

"He'll be fine. These guys are the small fish. The big fish is still swimming around," Hayden said.

Walking over to Salvadore, he spoke gently to the horse. Smelling someone known to him, the animal allowed him to come near. When Hayden tried to pet him, the stallion reared. They'd have to spend hours of retraining the horse. Hayden stepped back. "Now, we wait for the sheriff."

Chapter Twenty-Three

Hayden drained the last bit of coffee from his cup before setting it back on the table. He was taking a well-earned break from resettling the animals. He didn't want to dwell on the recent events, but images kept creeping into his mind. The fire was emblazoned in his memory. He'd been damned lucky. None of the horses were injured. There were damages, of course, but things worked out well.

"Why don't you catch a few hours' sleep?" Ginny's soft voice asked.

He pushed back his chair and stood. "Can't. Too much to do."

"Things will still get done without you for a few hours."

"Are you offering to join me? That would make the request much sweeter." He laughed at her elbow in his side. "Maybe when Monte wakes up."

A vehicle pulled up near the porch and a car door slammed. Hayden opened the door to find Jason Lancaster walking toward the porch. "What do you want, Lancaster?"

Dressed in a fine suit, the man looked like the proverbial used-car salesman, oily grin and all. "I just heard about the tragedy. Is everyone okay?"

Hayden wanted to snarl at the bastard but held his temper. "What tragedy? Just a little brushfire."

The man smirked. "Surely, the loss of your stallion warrants a little worry?"

"Don't know what you're talking about. Salvadore is in the barn." Hayden watched the other man's face closely. Shock flared in his eyes before his expression turned into a mask. "The grapevine must be slow. I came to offer my condolences. Losing your horse would be a terrible setback for your ranch."

"Get to the point, Lancaster. I've got work to do."

"I came to make you an offer. With all the problems you've had, cash must be tight. I'm willing to take half of the money owed me."

"That doesn't make good business sense. Why would you do such a thing?"

Jason shifted his stance. "I admire spunk and pulling this ranch out of the red takes that."

Hayden watched as the men by the barn stopped to watch. "And what about the lawsuit?"

"I'll drop it—no questions asked."

Hayden slanted him a disbelieving look as he came off the porch. "No deal. I'll take my chances with the court's decision."

"I'm not finished," Lancaster blustered.

"Neither am I." With a dismissive look, Hayden walked toward the barn. A string of curses followed by the slamming of a car door announced Lancaster's departure. "Show's over. Back to work," he told the men. Pulling on his gloves, he headed for the stud barn.

"Next time wake me up for the whole show." Monte said behind Hayden.

"That *was* a show, wasn't it? Did you see the part where I told him about Salvadore. For an instant, I saw real shock in his eyes."

Monte picked up a lariat and walked with him to Salvadore's stall. "Let's work him a little more today. We've got a long way back to where he was. A stud's no good if he's skittish."

Hayden laughed. "You would know."

****

Ginny watched the two men walk into the stud-barn. They would work with Salvadore all day. After this morning's show, she wondered how long Jason Lancaster would wait to make his big move. The fire and theft of the stallion were meant to be the turning point. She shuddered to think they could have lost everything last night. If Lancaster was willing to accept half his claim, it might settle the issue and they could get on with their lives. Too bad fifty-thousand-dollars didn't grow on trees.

Joining the others in the barn, she began her daily routine by releasing Rebecca from her stall and leading her into the arena. Anything to gain some normalcy. The mare was skittish after the hiatus of last night, so Ginny ran firm hands across her back and legs. Speaking sweet-nothings to the horse, she was able to coax her into her pacing routine. Ginny relaxed as she worked the mare through her paces.

"Losing the colt hasn't affected her beauty or grace," a low voice said behind her.

Deep into her work, Ginny startled and jerked the rope around Rebecca's neck. The horse jumped, kicking up her hind legs. Exasperated, she whirled around to face Hayden. "You can't sneak up on me like that. You startled the horse and broke her routine. Besides, aren't you supposed to be working Salvadore?"

"One of the perks of being boss. I work when and

where I want." Hayden pushed back his hat and wiped his forehead on his shirt sleeve. "Do you fancy a ride?"

Ginny gave him a disbelieving look. "Now? There's too much work to do."

"Another perk of the job. I get to say who works where and when. I really need to clear my head and could use a sounding board."

"Do I have a choice in this?"

Hayden leaned against the fence. His voice roughened. "With me, you always have a choice."

Ginny looked away from his heated gaze and pulled Rebecca in. "I'll saddle Brandy. She hasn't had any exercise today."

He pushed back from the fence, watching as she turned away. "By the way, bring your swimsuit—or not."

Ginny thought about Hayden's last words as she put the mare into her stall. She was lost either way. No swimsuit would prevent Hayden from making love to her. He could charm the pants off a saint. Heat rushed to her face at the thought. She quickly turned to Brandy's stall. With jerky movements she saddled the horse and led her outside.

An hour later, Ginny sat in the saddle, a tingle of excitement in her belly. A ride was just what she needed to calm her frayed nerves. She watched as Hayden approached, riding the big Palomino. "Where are we heading?" she asked as they rode toward the riding path.

"Let's decide as we go along. I'm in no hurry."

She bit back the words that automatically flew to her lips. Telling the boss how to do his job was suicidal. Not that she thought Hayden would fire her for speaking her mind. She decided to err on the side of caution. "You're the boss, "she said as she pushed her mount into a trot.

Ten minutes into the ride, Hayden turned to her. "I've been holding something back."

Ginny's heart plunged. Was this where he told her he'd lied about another woman in his life? Or was he hiding the fact that his feelings for her weren't real? She tipped her head and gave him a sober gaze. "Go on," she said, trying to keep the hurt from her voice.

"I didn't show you everything from the safety deposit box."

Ginny took a deep breath and tried to remain calm. "You don't have to share everything with me."

"Not as far as the business goes. There will be times when Monte and I will keep certain things quiet. What I've kept from you pertains to the ranch land."

Ginny's head swirled. Was there another danger to the ranch? "What do you mean?"

Hayden stopped his horse, pulling something from his pocket. He placed a small sack in her hand. "I've gone to Cheyenne and had these analyzed."

She poured the three, dull-gray rocks into her hand. Unaware of their significance, she wasn't impressed. "What is it?

"Silver."

The one word exploded in Ginny's mind. "What do you mean?

Hayden cleared his throat. "Austin found this silver and kept it hidden in his safety deposit box."

"Where did he find them?"

"That's the million-dollar question. I have a theory. Remember you said that Austin always came up with a little money when he needed it? I think he discovered the legendary mine. He scraped out enough of the ore to cover your expenses. He returned to the mine when he needed more money."

Ginny's heart raced. "If Austin had access to a silver mine, why in hell didn't he use it to fix up the ranch?"

Hayden shrugged. "Maybe he didn't want the ranch becoming a mining site. I have a feeling he wanted the ranch to stay the same. Though he did have ideas to expand. That's why he had the money saved in cash. He wanted to breed horses with a new stallion. I think time caught up to him."

Ginny thought back to the times when money appeared with no explanation. She had never questioned Austin as to its origin. "Did he leave any clues to where he found the silver?"

"He left a vague map. I'm sure the mine is in the South-West corner of the property. Think about it. We use all the other areas. Someone would have stumbled onto the mine by now if it were close to the homestead and walking trails."

"May I see the map? I know the ranch like the back of my hand. I'll find it."

"This has to remain quiet for now," Hayden cautioned. "Lancaster must have someone close to the ranch on his payroll. I don't want them to get wind of this."

Ginny's mind tingled with anticipation. "Got it. Are we going to look for the mine today?"

Hayden grinned and pulled a small, folded paper from his pocket. "Damned right we are. I only recognize Teardrop Lake by its shape. Nothing is labeled." He handed the paper to her.

Wiping her sweaty hands across her jeans, she took the scrap and carefully unfolded it. Studying the map from several angles, she finally oriented the map where Teardrop Lake was in the correct direction. "Looks like it is between the Far Paddock and the Flats. That's a lot of territory. We'll never cover it in one day."

"That's okay. I'm fine with taking our time and keeping it quiet. We can't even let the hands know what we're doing. Let's just do a quick perimeter of the area to get an idea of what we're facing." Hayden nudged Trigger forward and moved closer beside Ginny.

She shifted in the saddle to face him. "Careful. People might get ideas if you come any closer."

With an unexpected swoop, Hayden pulled her into an embrace. "Good. If they're sidetracked by our closeness, they won't be so nosy about where we're riding."

Ginny's heart raced. She forgot all about the ranch and the mine as his lips plundered hers. The horses bumped and pulled them apart. She wanted to grab him and pull him back. Instead, she picked up her reins and moved to take the lead.

Chapter Twenty-Four

Hayden swallowed the last sip of coffee and pushed back his chair. Coffee seemed to be what he needed to get through the pile of paperwork. The phone rang as he was heading for the kitchen. He thought of adding a coffee pot to the office decor but answered the ringing phone with a longing look at the empty cup. "Hello?"

"Jake Bannister here."

"Hello, sheriff. What can I do for you today?"

"I wanted to fill you in on what's happened since you caught Jeffrey McCallister and his partner, Rick. Both men are singing like birds. We don't have enough to charge Lancaster yet, but we can bring him in for questioning. I'm sure I can break him."

"That's great news. If you need any help, let me know. I've broken a few bastards in my time."

"I bet you have," the sheriff said.

Hayden hung up the land line. Immediately, his cell phone buzzed. Caller ID informed him that it was his Cheyenne lawyer. He felt his gut tighten. Depending on what the court decided, he could face a substantial set back. "Hey, Peter. I hope you have good news."

"Sort of good news. The judge ruled that since Ginny's great-grandmother was married in a native ceremony, she broke the marriage when she went back to her people. This means that none of her heirs, like Ginny, have a claim to the property."

Hayden felt a touch of guilt. It didn't seem fair that Ginny had been left out by Austin. "What about Lancaster's claim?"

"The judge called a recess until tomorrow at noon. He needs more time to study the documents."

"So we wait again," Hayden said.

"I've got a good feeling about it," Peter Rayburn said and hung up.

Hayden stared at his phone as if waiting for advice on how to break this to Ginny. She said she wasn't interested, but he knew in his heart she was. Her people. like other tribes, had suffered as white men moved into their territory and took their land. History was being repeated. With a sigh he stood and, bypassing the coffee pot, went to find Ginny.

She wasn't hard to find, considering she spent every waking moment with the horses. He stood by the arena fence and watched quietly as she worked the Appaloosa. Keeping her word, she had Ryan in the ring also. He wasn't too worried. Ginny could make horses do things that most people only dreamed about. He admired the way she was breaking the animal to the saddle. Most men would jump on the horse and let it buck until it became docile. Hayden thought it took the soul out of the horse. He wanted the mustangs to remain true to their breed. Their wild spirit was exactly a match to his plans for Salvadore.

Ginny handed Rebecca's reins to Ryan. "Take her. I need to talk to Hayden,"

"She's made fast progress," said Hayden.

Ginny pulled up a bale of hay and sat. "She's the reason we need to talk."

Hayden reached for another bale. "Is something

wrong with the Appaloosa?"

"She's doing beautifully. She tries me some time, but we get along. When are you going to give the poor thing a name?"

"Naming an animal is something special. It takes time waiting and watching while she trains. One day you'll look at her and recognize her spirit. That's when you can give her a name."

"Are you sure you're not Native? You keep talking about souls and spirits—next thing you know, you'll hold a special naming ceremony."

Hayden smiled. "Mock me if you will. Deep down, you know I'm right."

"We're cutting it close if we want foals this spring."

Hayden watched color bloom on her cheeks. He supposed being the only woman on a ranch had its drawbacks. "Don't get all shy on me. You'll be expected to be in the barn with Edith.

"I'm always in the barn. I've seen horses couple before."

"It can get a little intense. I won't fault you for being a little hesitant. Be advised, the men will be sent home as soon as the matings are over. I might even seek the lake for a cold swim."

She placed her palm against his chest. "We could always take a swim together."

"Now, you're talking, darling."

Ginny stood and turned to leave.

"Hold on." He watched as she sat back down. It was obvious she was uncomfortable. "Do you have the records of their cycles? We'll use those to get the horses scheduled. I will want the Appaloosa first so, get her ready."

When he began to talk horses, Ginny looked more at ease. "All the records are in the file cabinet. Rebecca will be ready by the end of the week."

Hayden's eyes narrowed. "What would I do without you?

Her lips curved into a smile. "Figure things out on your own. You have an uncanny knack for doing so."

"Part of my SEAL training. Things always went wrong, and we had to think on the run."

"It goes deeper than that. It's as if you can sense the horses' feelings."

He laughed. "Now, who's going all spiritual?"

"Don't, Hayden. Making light of a gift is wrong. We're each given certain talents. We should use them to their full advantage."

He eased forward, his breath fanning her neck. "I've got talents that need using."

She leaned back into his embrace.

His lips traced a path on her velvety skin from nape to her delicate ear. "Interested?"

She pulled from his embrace. "I've got to get busy. The boss might catch us goofing off."

"He did," Monte said.

Hayden moved back from her. "You need to work on your timing. I was just delivering a message."

"I need your help with Salvadore. Coming?"

Hayden groaned and winked at Ginny. "I'll be right there." He dropped a light kiss on her cheek and headed for the stud barn. His conscience hurt. He hadn't told Ginny about the lawyer's call.

Chapter Twenty-Five

Hayden dragged his feet as he entered the house. It had been a long day since his conversation with his Cheyenne lawyer and he'd not yet told Ginny what Peter said. Dirt covered him from toe to head, leaving his hair a sandy brown. All he wanted was a beer and a bath. He ignored the urge to bypass the kitchen and sneak in the back. Facing Ginny was going to be hard, but it had to be done.

"Hey, Hayden. Want a piece?" Ginny indicated the apples she was cutting up for a pie.

"No thanks. I'll wait for the finished product. Where's Noel?"

Ginny continued slicing the apples. "She had a doctor's appointment, so I took over."

"Are you at a stopping point? I need to see you in the office."

Pausing the knife's motion, Ginny asked, "Is something wrong?"

Hayden gave her a look that was both encouraging and confusing. "Yes and no."

Ginny raised her brow but received no response from Hayden. "I can finish this in about ten minutes. Will that do?"

Hayden heard the question in her voice. Why had he been so cryptic? It was a conversation like any other they might have. He nodded and went up the stairs. His new bedroom took up the entire width of the attic, giving him room for a king-sized bed. He looked longingly at the navy coverlet and sighed. Wasting no more time, he showered and donned clean clothes. Now, he felt more like facing Ginny. He'd barely settled into the desk chair before a knock sounded at the door. "Come in."

Ginny's head appeared around the door. "I only have an hour before I have to start dinner."

He pulled the second chair closer to the desk. "This won't take that long."

She sat and waited for him to speak.

He almost wavered when he looked into her vulnerable face. Clearing his throat, he spoke. "I got a call from Peter."

"That's the lawyer in Cheyenne, right?"

"Yes. They don't have a final decision yet on Lancaster's claim, but they did in the case of the marriage between Austin and your grandmother. The judge ruled that since it was a Cheyenne ceremony, your grandmother severed the marriage when she returned to her people."

"That is the traditional way for a divorce. If she had lived with her people, she would have been sent back to her relatives."

Hayden ginned. "Sounds practical and economical to me."

Ginny looked grim. "It prevents the need for reparations to a wife. So, if you're a wife it's not very equitable."

"I'm sorry. For then and now. Today, reparations to women come only after a fight. Your grandmother should have been compensated and you should have had the right to inherit."

"It's all right, Hayden. I had little expectation of the will being overturned. In truth, I'm glad it's over."

Hayden reached out and softly cupped her face. "One day it will change."

"I sure hope so. Now, can I go check on the pie?"

"You're making two, right?"

"Yes, One for the guys, and one for us."

"Good. Now, that I'm clean, I'm going to work on office stuff."

She left without another word and Hayden locked the door. Taking out the things from the safety deposit box, he spread them on the desk. He pushed the gun, letter and cash aside. Picking up the sack and small folded paper he opened the bag and unfolded the paper. The silver ore was nondescript and would be hard to recognize for its value. He supposed his Great-grandfather had been a careful and resourceful man. He'd have been hard too. He had no compunction about leaving Ginny penniless. People didn't hold on to a ranch this size for as long as he did without being hard. He would have faced his share of hardships and danger and given as good as he got.

Damn, he wished he could have met the man. They wouldn't have agreed on much, but they had the same drive. On a whim he put the rocks in his pocket along with the map and headed for the stables. Trigger was eager to be ridden and he tried to settle him with an apple. After a few minutes he saddled the stallion and hopped on. The horse took off at a trot and Hayden had to use a heavy hand to keep him in check. Soon, he passed the lake and headed for the Southwest part of the ranch.

Chapter Twenty-Six

Trigger settled down as Hayden looked for the mine. Unfortunately, he had no idea what it would look like. Since it hadn't been found by anyone, he suspected it was simply a hole in the ground—and there was a lot of ground. Ginny hadn't said anything about people searching this area. That meant he had a possibility of stumbling across the mine. If he didn't get himself killed first.

The people who had caused the problems on the ranch were in jail but there was Lancaster himself. He wouldn't put it past the bastard to trespass on Wilcoyt property with a long-range-rifle in hand. The thought sent a shiver down his back, and he turned to check the woods behind him. Nothing. He continued up and down the few hills, any one of which could hold the entrance to the mine. Dammit, there wasn't any *proof* that the mine existed.

The sound of water drifted to his ears. Thinking Trigger could use a drink, he wandered in that direction. A little stream ran down a slope and curved off into the trees. He dismounted and led the horse to the stream. When the horse had finished drinking, he took a swig from his canteen. The tepid water did little to quench his thirst. Bending down, he splashed water over his face and head, enjoying the coolness.

"Well, Trigger, this is the part where you're

supposed to point me in the right direction by nodding your head." He stared at the oblivious horse and then looked up the little hill ahead. "It looks as good a place as any," he said jokingly. Tying the horse to a bush, he moved up the hill on foot. When he reached the top, he looked out at the landscape. Ginny would like it here. Maybe she would build her cabin here. "Not if I can help it. She's going to live with me."

Arrogant as it sounded, he meant every word. She was his—not like a possession, but an equal partner. Why the hell hadn't he proposed to her yet? He thought about what she might say to his proposal. Disgruntled at the thought, he took a step back to get a better look at a shadow a few feet away. He stepped on a rotten branch. A loud crack rent the air and he fell backwards. The hole was covered by straw and dead leaves. His weight pushed through the plant cover, and he fell into a very deep hole. The fact barely registered as another crack sounded. He jerked in pain as his leg snapped and he fell against the rocky floor. He'd been shot, stabbed and nearly blown up, yet this pain superseded all those wounds.

His vision dimmed but he hung on to consciousness. Something niggled at his brain, but he had trouble grasping it. He heard a bird sing above him, and a chill covered his skin. Not even that bird knew he was down here. That was it—his phone. Patting his pocket he failed to come up with it. He stifled a scream and ran his hands outward around his body. His hand touched a large rock and then his cell. Hayden's heart raced as he held it up in front of his eyes. Filtered light showed the cell screen. Cracked glass cut his hand and he dropped the phone. Picking it up again, he pushed the buttons, and nothing happened. His heart dropped. The phone was dead. Just like he would be if he didn't get out of here.

He did scream, then, followed by a long string of colorful curses. He forced himself to calm. He'd been in worse circumstances than this and had made it out. Only this time, he'd told no one he was going out or where he was going. He'd had friends to help him before and they'd do so now. When he didn't show up for supper, Ginny would come looking for him. She might guess what he was doing and that something had gone wrong.

"All right, "he spoke aloud. "I'll yell her name every twenty minutes. Maybe she'll hear me. Ginny!"

****

Ginny pulled the second pie from the oven and smiled. Hayden was going to love it. Where was he? Normally, he'd be washing up by now. Adam, Cooper and Monte came in and washed up at the sink. " Have you guys seen Hayden?"

"No, he must be upstairs, "said Monte. "I haven't seen him all day."

"That's strange. He's normally here by now."

Hayden was still absent by the time all the hands had sat down for supper. Ginny began to worry in earnest. Her mind kept playing scenarios and all made her feel scared. Had another snake caused his horse to throw him? Was he having another flashback? Uneasy, she pulled off her apron and headed for the door.

"Hey, what's up?" Ryan called.

She pulled the door open. "I'm worried about Hayden."

"Why don't you just call him? Cooper asked.

"Now, why didn't I think of that." Her words came out sarcastic because she *had* called him. Twice. He hadn't answered either time. She'd thought of any number of reasons why he might not answer but none satisfied her.

Monte stood. "Because she's already called him. When was the last time you saw him?"

"About two. I was just putting the first pie in the oven."

"Have any of you guys seen him?" Monte asked.

After a round of "Nos" from the group, Monte looked at his watch. "It's five-thirty. He should have been here by now."

"His truck is here," Cooper observed.

Monte joined Ginny by the door. "Adam, go check to see if his horse is here. He might have gone for a ride."

Ginny was glad she had someone here. She followed Adam out the door. "I'll saddle up if his horse is gone."

"I can send up the drone. If he's out riding, I'll find him," Peyton said as he scurried off.

Adam met them halfway between the house and the barn. "His horse is gone."

Ginny tried to remain calm, but her heart raced. Something had to be wrong. "We have about two hours of daylight left. I'll lead the search party." Monte gave her a look that had her spine stiffening. "Don't bother to tell me to stay. I'll just go anyway. Besides, I know the property better than anyone."

Monte threw up his hands. "You're right."

"Bring some equipment and the SUV. If he's hurt, we'll need it." Ginny directed everyone giving quick, precise directions. The men anticipated most of the commands she gave and within fifteen minutes, they were ready to leave.

"Wait, I've got to tell you something. Hayden may

not be on the property you're familiar with. We were keeping it a secret, but he may be on the Southwest section of the property. None of you have been there. We suspect the infamous lost mine may be there."

"Okay," Monte drawled. "Secret means we can't call in the sheriff or others. We damn sure don't want strangers crawling around all looking for the mine instead of Hayden. What about Mustang? We could use a tracker."

Peyton spoke up. "He just called. Said something about a feeling. Sometimes that man scares me."

Ginny's body felt numb and jacked up at the same time. "Peyton, would you saddle another horse for Mustang." She rubbed her hands against her pant leg, trying to feel something. Why hadn't she told Hayden how she felt? If he.... she reined in her thoughts. They were going to find him, and he'd be fine.

Mustang pulled his truck in beside them and jumped out before the wheels stopped. Ginny ran forward and buried her head against the big man's chest. "I have a bad feeling. You've got to find him."

"Is he riding Trigger?"

"Yes, why?"

"There's a tiny notch in the front left shoe. If we find tracks, we'll be able to tell it's him.

"Good. Let's go." Ginny was up on her horse without another word.

Leading his horse by the rein, Mustang stopped often to check for tracks. After some time, he mounted and headed for the training trail.

"How does he tell yesterday's tracks from today's?" Monte asked as he rode beside Ginny.

"That's a secret my uncle has never shared. He likes

to keep the mystical aura around what he does."

Monte cuffed her on the arm. "He's going to be all right."

"Don't. I know all the accident's that can happen on a ranch. What if Lancaster came after him?"

Monte straightened in his saddle. "Hayden can handle a man like Lancaster and a few of his minions, too. He doesn't even have to be armed to be able to come out on top."

"I'm scared," Ginny said just above a whisper.

"We all are. He's, my brother. He belongs to all of us guys. I'm going to think positive until I have a need to worry." He cast a sideways look at her. "Does he know how you feel?"

Ginny's gaze flew to Monte's questioning eyes. "Probably not."

Monte threw back his head and laughed. "You're probably right. Hayden doesn't think he deserves to be happy. I hope you intend to dissuade him of that complex."

"There are a number of things I intend to—"

"Here are some fresh tracks." Mustang stood and brushed the sand from his knees. "These were made today. They're leading to the lake."

"That's the only way he knows. If he's going where I think he is, he'll turn left at the lake."

With a nod, Mustang mounted up, and moved forward.

The light was beginning to fade when Ginny thought she heard a sound. "Wait. I heard something."

Everyone stopped and listened. No one heard anything. Slowly, they crept forward pausing often to listen.

"Ginny, I love you! Will you marry me?"

The loud shout came from nearby and she had to reel in before she galloped forward. "Hayden? Where are you?"

The yelling stopped. They moved closer to where the sound had emanated.

Mustang dismounted and the others followed his lead.

Tying her horse to a bush, Ginny walked forward cautiously. Why didn't he say something? "Why does his voice sound odd?" she asked.

"It sounds like he's inside a well," Mustang said.

"You mean…?"

"I'm not sure what I mean. Let's just move slowly. Give him a call. Maybe he'll answer."

Ginny swallowed, took a deep breath, then called out, "Hayden? Where are you?"

"I'm here! Be careful, there's a hole."

Everyone laughed, easing the tension.

"Keep talking so we can find you," Mustang yelled.

"What's your answer?" His voice floated toward her. He sounded tired and something else. Pain. He was hurt.

"Yes, I will," she called. Are you hurt, Hayden?"

The men spread out, walking toward his voice.

"Yeah, I am."

His voice sounded so matter of fact, she grinned. He must be in a lot of pain to have admitted it

"Did you bring a light? It's pretty dark down here."

The voice sounded just to her right. At the same time a horse whinnied. There was Trigger standing patiently down the little hill. Ginny rushed forward, nearly falling in the process. Mustang caught her arm and pulled her back.

"We're here," she yelled.

Monte stepped up and shone the lamp over the hole. Over to the right, the light picked out Hayden lying with his left leg at an awkward angle. "You're not supposed to take the afternoon off and snooze."

"Hey, buddy. I think my leg's broken and I'm not alone down here."

"What do you mean you're not alone?" Monte asked.

"There's a dead body; well actually it's a skeleton. A man by the clothing. He's holding a saddle bag."

"I bet it's the money from the robbed stagecoach," Ginny squealed.

"How about you guys get me out of here and we'll discuss the elephant in the room later," Hayden said.

Monte looked at Ginny and she nodded. Handing one end of the rope to Monte and Peyton, she eased down the rope to the floor. Her headlamp quickly highlighted Hayden lying on his back. She bent to assess the damage. "Is your leg the only part that is hurt?"

"I have a busted lip. Want to kiss it better?"

"You're shameless."

"I am. Do you have to put the leg in place before you get me out of here?"

"Let me take a closer look."

The med-kit came down beside her on a rope. Ginny ran a gentle hand down the broken leg. Her heart ached for Hayden's pain. Reaching for the kit, she noticed that it wasn't the one she'd put in the SUV. Opening it she found a doctor's complete kit including medications."

Monte slid down beside her as the entire area lit up from work lights on a stand. "Let me cut that pant leg and we can give him a shot for the pain."

"I agree. I also think that it's best to pad the leg

without repositioning it. He's looking at a pin at least."

Monte chuckled. "It'll match the rest of them. Our boy is a little worse for wear."

Ginny called up to the men above her. "Send down some blankets, pillows or whatever you have to cushion his leg." She looked at Monte. "You don't happen to have a stretcher in the SUV, do you?"

"No, but the boys will make one. Stretcher," he called up to Adam.

"Already made one. Watch it. It's on the way down," Cooper said as he eased the makeshift stretcher down into the hole.

Monte grabbed the scissors and cut off the bottom leg of Hayden's pants.

Ginny handed him a pre-filled syringe and he injected the pain killer into the meaty part of Hayden's thigh.

Hayden cursed and Ginny placed her hand on his cheek. "That's it. It won't hurt so bad now."

Hayden placed a kiss into her palm. "Honey, you saying yes to my proposal, makes everything better."

"Come on guys. More important stuff right now," Monte complained. "I need you to go up now, Ginny."

She flashed Monte a questioning look. "But—"

"It'll be easier on him when I transfer him."

Realizing he had Hayden's best interests at heart, she acquiesced and stepped into the rope harness. The guys pulled her up and she waited anxiously as the men worked together to get Hayden out of the hole and into the SUV.

She gave a now sweating Hayden a quick kiss. "I'm driving."

When no one argued, Ginny took off.

Chapter Twenty-Seven

The smell of antiseptic burned Ginny's nose as she walked down the hospital corridor. Though days had passed, the scent always made her cringe. She turned the corner, surprised to see Hayden, sitting in the hall, talking on someone's cell phone. His laughter floated to her, and she smiled. It had been five long days since the accident. She'd tried to spend more time at the hospital, but Hayden had nixed that idea."

"You heard right. Ginny is in charge while I'm gone." Hayden's words nearly stopped her in her tracks. His words sounded so strange to her ears. No one had ever put her in charge of anything. She found that she liked the idea. "One of the perks, I work when I want and where I want." Ginny repeated the words he said a few weeks ago.

"I'm in trouble, you're spouting my own words back at me."

"Who were you talking to that made you laugh?"

"Only the sheriff. He wanted more access to the 'crime scene.' You must have put a bee in his bonnet. He's trying to figure a legal way to get back to the hole. I've decided to call the mine, The Hole in One."

"What mine?" Ginny's grin threatened to burst into laughter.

"Since the deal I worked out with the Black Rock Mining Company. I contacted them as soon as I could think straight. By the way, I didn't get a kiss."

Ginny bent to swipe a gentle kiss on his lips. Hayden grabbed her, pulling her into a hard embrace. "We're in public and you don't even have on pants."

Hayden held her hand. "That's the way I like it. Not that you have anything to worry about with my leg and all."

"It's not your leg that's the problem, Hayden. It's this place. I refuse to make love to you with the smell of antiseptic in my nose. I can't wait until you come home."

"Well, young lady, you've got your wish," Hayden's doctor said from behind her. "I'm releasing him as soon as the paperwork is complete."

"Great, I'll call your chariot. You'll be more comfortable in the SUV," Ginny said as she pulled out her phone.

The doctor handed her a list of discharge instructions and prescriptions for pain meds. "He's not going to be an easy patient. He'll have home health come out three times a week and you'll need to take him to therapy as soon as it starts."

Ginny suddenly felt overwhelmed. How was she going to take care of Hayden and run the ranch at the same time?

"It's going to be all right, sweetheart," he said as if he read her mind. "Since the judge dismissed Lancaster's case as fraudulent, the mine has been found, and you've agreed to marry me, we're in for some good times. You still want to marry me, right?"

"Suddenly, everything looks clear. I love you and definitely want to marry you. Once you can ride again, we'll set the date."

"No, once I can walk again, we'll do the deed.

Agreed?" Hayden murmured.

"I agree." Ginny said.

"Hot damn. Get that in writing, Hayden." Monte stood behind them grinning. "The nurse gave me a head's up, and I brought the SUV."

"Great, let's blow this place." Hayden laughed.

Much later as Hayden and Ginny sat on the porch watching the stars, Hayden asked her a question. "Ginny, I love you so much. Will you love honor and cherish me until death us do part?"

She stood and moved to his wheelchair. It's time for bed, Hayden."

"I can't get up the stairs."

"You're right. You'll have to sleep with me. I'll give you my answer in bed."

"He pulled her in for a hard kiss. "I bet you will."

Ginny took a deep breath of air as she came up from his kiss. Her heartbeat twice its normal speed. "

"I bet you're right."

A word about the author...

Evelyn Timidaiski is a Golden Palm winner, Winter Rose finalist, and author of the new series Brandon's Brigade. Her sense of adventure, deep-rooted values, and love of romance enliven her fast-paced novels. Ms. Timidaiski lives with her Pomeranian, Chloe, in Mississippi, where she writes romantic suspense, contemporary, and fantasy. When she isn't painting or taking nature photographs, you will find her at her computer, crafting her newest novel. She loves to hear from readers.

You can visit her online at her website http://www.evelyntimidaiskiauthor.com/ or find her on Facebook at http://www.evelyntimidaiskiauthor.com/

Thank you for purchasing
this publication of The Wild Rose Press, Inc.

For questions or more information
contact us at
info@thewildrosepress.com.

The Wild Rose Press, Inc.
www.thewildrosepress.com